A SAVAGE DOPEBOY

Lock Down Publications and Ca$h
Presents
A Savage Dopeboy
A Novel by *Ghost*

Lock Down Publications
P.O. Box 870494
Mesquite, Tx 75187

Visit our website @
www.lockdownpublications.com

Lock Down Publications
Like our page on Facebook: Lock Down Publications @
www.facebook.com/lockdownpublications.ldp
Cover design and layout by: **Dynasty Cover Me**
Book interior design by: **Shawn Walker**
Edited by: **Shawnon Corprew**

Stay Connected with Us!

Text **LOCKDOWN** to 22828 to stay up-to-date with new releases, sneak peaks, contests and more…

Thank you.

Submission Guideline.

Submit the first three chapters of your completed manuscript to ldpsubmissions@gmail.com, subject line: Your book's title. The manuscript must be in a .doc file and sent as an attachment. Document should be in Times New Roman, double spaced and in size 12 font. Also, provide your synopsis and full contact information. If sending multiple submissions, they must each be in a separate email.

Have a story but no way to send it electronically? You can still submit to LDP/Ca$h Presents. Send in the first three chapters, written or typed, of your completed manuscript to:

LDP: Submissions Dept
Po Box 870494
Mesquite, Tx 75187

DO NOT send original manuscript. Must be a duplicate.

Provide your synopsis and a cover letter containing your full contact information.

Only if your submission is **approved**, will you then get a response letter.

Thanks for considering LDP and Ca$h Presents.

Dedications:

First of all, this book is dedicated to my Baby Girl 3/10, the love of my life and purpose for everything I do. As long as I'm alive, you'll never want nor NEED for anything. We done went from flipping birds to flipping books. The best is yet to come.

To LDP'S CEO- Ca$h & COO- Shawn:

I would like to thank y'all for this opportunity. The wisdom, motivation, and encouragement that I've received from you two is greatly appreciated.

The grind is real. The loyalty in this family is real. I'm riding with LDP 'til the wheels fall off.

THE GAME IS OURS!

I GOT THE STREETS!

Ghost

Chapter 1

Reggie took a long swallow from his pink Sprite and ran his hand across his lips. He curled his upper lip as he watched Babygirl smile seductively, and bite onto her bottom lip, as she locked eyes with T. *The fuck is goin' between her and this stud. 'Cuz MY bitch, know better,* he thought. Reggie was sure they'd been secretly flirting all night long. It was making him uneasy and he did his best to mask his anger.

Babygirl felt T's hand creep onto her thigh. She was trying her best to not let on as to what was taking place underneath the table. Her man was sitting right across from her, and he had a horrible temper. She felt they were flirting harmlessly. They had been doing it ever since they were kids and he was more like a distant brother. T had two sons by her best friend, Star, and she'd never cross her by fucking her man behind her back.

He stood about 6 feet, light skinned, with hazel eyes and curly hair. Physically, he was definitely her type. Mixed with the fact he was a boss, he was often tempting.

Reggie retwisted the cap back on his Sprite and looked across the table. They had been playing dominos, as the pieces were still in the middle of the table connected to each other. They also had glasses of Patron and half-smoked blunts that had been put out because they'd been blowing heavily for six hours straight. Reggie scooted his chair all the way back from the table and bounced up, startling T and Babygirl.

Reggie frowned, and sat his bottle on the table, feeling the effects of the lean taking over him. "Say, Babygirl, let me holla at you in this room back here." He looked like he was ready to fall over. He rocked back and forth, then caught himself, pressing hard on the balls of his feet.

Babygirl exhaled loudly. "Look, Reggie, I ain't on that shit tonight. I'm just trying to chill with our people. So I'm finna go back here and holla at you, but if you get on that dumb shit, I'm out." She said and stood up, scooting her chair back with her big ass booty. She had on some real tight Fendi jean coochie cutters that were all in her ass. Her thighs were thick, and her waist was slim. She had the body of a top-notch, money-making stripper. That was her profession, and she took it to heart. Her goal was to be the number one feature stripper in Atlanta, and so far, her name was ringing more than a bell on top of a church.

T gazed down at her ass and shook his head. Babygirl had him ready to fuck her and if given the chance, he would have worn her ass out. He had respect for his right-hand man, but he'd put that respect on the table to fuck her thick ass. Plus, the word was already out that Reggie's dick was smaller than a tater tot, so he couldn't understand why Babygirl hadn't left him yet.

Reggie saw where his eyes were and mugged T. "Damn, nigga, you all in my bitch's ass. What's good?" He spat, wiping his mouth.

T stood up and smiled. "Nigga, I ain't finna get on that shit wit' you. Every time you get to drinking that shit, you act like you want that fire. I'm finna grab my bitch, and we outta here. I'll holla at you in the morning, so we can bust that move. That's 50 G's, nigga, so get this fuck shit out yo' system." He walked past him and bumped him.

Reggie wanted to say something to him but stayed silent. He figured he'd just take it out on Babygirl, and he was planning on fucking her up good. He was tired of her trying him. He knew T had hands, and he just didn't feel like going through all of that. He felt he could whoop Babygirl's ass with no effort.

Two minutes later, he stood mugging Babygirl in the kitchen when T walked past them with his arm around Star.

Star was fucked up. "Girl, I'll see y'all asses tomorrow. I'm finna go get me some dick before the babysitter drops my kids off. Have a good night."

She stumbled out of the door, being held up by her man. Star was just as thick as Babygirl. She was a stripper, too, and she made a nice lump sum every night.

T paused at the door and turned around, looking Babygirl in the eye. "You hold yo' head, shorty. Bruh get to acting crazy, hit my phone." He said seriously. Babygirl nodded her head.

"Alright, y'all be safe." T paused for a minute and looked Reggie up and down.

He already knew Reggie was finna get on some bullshit. If Reggie's brother, Jock, didn't damn near run Atlanta, he didn't think they'd be as cool as they were. He felt like he was bitch made. He shook his head. "50 G's, nigga."

Reggie mugged him before nodding and closed the door behind him. He gave Babygirl the look of her death.

Babygirl walked past him heading to their bedroom. "What you wanna talk to me about? I'm tired, and I gotta be at work later on tonight, so let's make this shit snappy." She didn't feel like dealing with Reggie that night. She had to mentally get herself together so she could go out and make her money so they could move out of her mother's house by the end of the month as planned.

She couldn't understand how Reggie's brother was running a whole side of Atlanta, and he was still broke. The majority of the financial responsibilities fell on her. That shit got tiring after a while. She felt she should have been able to lean on her man for support, but she knew better than that.

She stepped into the room and sat on the bed, waiting for his burdensome ass to step through the door.

Reggie took a deep breath as he closed the door behind him and locked it. *Wham!* He cocked back,and punched her straight in the mouth, so hard that she flew backward on the bed, holding her face. He jumped on the bed, straddling her, and smacked her with an open hand. *Whap!*

"Bitch! You think it's sweet? You think I won't get in this ass?" *Whap!*

Babygirl had never seen this side of him before. He'd never laid a hand on her before. She felt blood dripping from her chin. He grabbed her by her hair delivering a smack to her face again, twice as hard. Whap!

She tried break free from grip. "Get off of me, Reggie! Please! I didn't even do anything!"

Reggie grimaced. There was nothing like beating the shit out of a woman. It was like food to his soul. He loved how afterward, they always bowed down in submission.

He grabbed her by the leg and dragged her off the bed onto the floor, kicking her in the chest, knocking the wind out of her. He grabbed another handful of her hair, and punched her in the face, busting her nose wide open causing it to bleed. He took his jagged pinky ring and dragged it across her pretty face, lacerating the skin.

"You thought I didn't peep yo' hoe ass smiling at my nigga? Walking around this ma'fucka like you run shit just 'cuz you bring in a few more pennies than I do. Well, bitch, what's this?" He pushed her to the floor, stepping on her back as he flipped the mattress over, and threw four kilos of heroin on her back.

Babygirl attempted to take a deep breath but winced from the pain that he'd inflicted. Her vision was hazy. She felt helpless.

"I'm finna be eating, bitch. That's what you wanna see, huh? You wanna see me eating so yo' gold digging ass can spend it all? Huh, bitch?" He grabbed her by the throat and started to squeeze. He had thoughts of killing her and getting a new bitch, but he wasn't one of the type of niggas who could just leave. He had to get rid of a person. He had a few bodies under his belt. .

Boom! Boom! Boom! There was beating on the door. "Hey, what y'all doing in there? Is y'all fighting? Y'all betta not be fighting in my house! Babygirl? Babygirl?" It was Linda, Babygirl's mom. Fuck, Reggie thought.

Reggie choked her even harder before replying. "Go lay yo' ass down, old lady! I got this shit in here. I'm putting *my* bitch in her place. You ain't got shit to do with this." He growled and smacked Babygirl with all of his might.

"Momma! Help me!"

Pow!

Linda fell down to her knees as she continue to pound on the door, wailing at the top of her lungs. "Reggie, what did you do to my baby? Babygirl? Babygirl? Answer me!"

* * *

Jahrome pulled the all-black, 1964 Impala to the curb before hitting the switch to put the roof back in place. He had a 9 millimeter on his lap, and a thick ass Puerto Rican from the north side in his passenger's seat. She worked with his sister, Babygirl, at the club. They met three weeks prior, and he'd been wearing that ass out ever since. Her nose was wide open already, and he knew this would be beneficial for him. He turned off the ignition, and turned to look at her.

Mami licked her lips and smiled at Jahrome. He was rocking the brand new True Religion outfit she'd bought him the day before, with the matching custom-made Jordans. His waves were popping, and his face was lined up. In her opinion, he was one of the finest black men that she had ever seen, and his dick game was crazy. At first, she didn't even think she could take all of him, but he did some shit with his tongue that got her ready to fuck a million niggas if she had to. She was in love.

"Why you looking at me like that? " He asked, squeezing her thick thighs. He was ready to hit that pussy, and get her to talking Spanish while she moaned at the top of her lungs. That Spanish shit drove him crazy when he was deep inside her.

She opened her Birkin bag, and pulled out a wad of hundreds totaling 10 thousand dollars. "I got this lil' chump change here, *papi*. Since I know you in the streets, I want you to take it and make something happen. I should be able to hit you with this amount again when I get back from touring in Miami this weekend. I'm hella booked down there."

She lowered her head and looked up at him with those sexy bedroom eyes. They were mesmerizing to everyone else but him. Jahrome was all about his paper first.

Growing up with his sister, Babygirl, she had always kept bad ass buddies around, so he was used to pretty faces. Most of her friends were used to getting by on their looks, and that disgusted him. He was more attracted to women who made shit happen: go-getters, hustlers, lone wolves, and trendsetters who thought outside of the box. Mami had that potential, so she had him intrigued.

He took the bundle from her, just as he saw his mother running down the steps of her house, and straight over to his car, beating on the windshield.

"Baby! Baby! Help! He's in there beating your sister to death! He gon' kill her! Please make him stop!" She hollered before dropping to the ground and shaking uncontrollably.

Jahrome's heart beat intensely in his chest. He opened the door to the car, and ran around it, dropping to his knees hard.

"Momma! Momma!" He put his ear to her chest and listened for her heart. It was still beating hard.

Mami jumped out of the car, picked his gun up, and handed it to him. "Jahrome, go make sure my homegirl is good. I'll get her right. Go, *papi!*" She knelt down and took his mother into her arms.

* * *

Reggie slapped Babygirl again, but she was knocked out and losing large amounts of blood. He didn't give a fuck. In his mind, that was what a bitch deserved when she got out of order. He flung her to the floor and wiped his mouth with the back of his hand before standing up and lighting a cigarette.

The bedroom door flew in, and Jahrome fell through it like a fucking animal. He took the door and threw it to the side. He saw his sister on the floor in a puddle of blood, and his vision got cloudy. He had to terminate this nigga.

Chapter 2

Reggie dropped down, and slid his hand under the bed, coming up with a .38 special. He cocked it back and busted it with no hesitation. *Boom!*

The bullet hit Jahrome's shoulder and knocked him back a few steps. His anger had gotten the best of him, and out of ignorance, he ducked down and dived at Reggie, landing on top of him. He punched him repeatedly in the face with all of his might. He could feel the man's bones breaking under his fist. He had his knees planted on the wrist that held the gun, and he gave him one haymaker after the next.

Reggie started crying like a baby. He could hear his face cracking under Jahrome's fists.

"Bitch ass nigga! I told you about hitting my sister! I told you I don't honor that shit! I told you I don't like pussy niggas who hit women! Now, I'm finna kill you, on my momma! I'm finna kill you!"

He aimed for the bridge of his nose and broke it easily. He took the heel of his hand and slammed it upward with all of his might. Jahrome continued to beat his face in, blow after blow.

He imagined the nigga beating his sister. He imagined Babygirl crying out for him. He wasn't there because he'd fucking off with Mami. It was his job to protect her. It was his job to protect both of the women in his family, because nobody else would. Their father had left a long time ago to chase the mighty needle of heroin.

Reggie's face was a bloody pulp, yet Jahrome continued to deliver blow after blow. He felt like he failed his sister.

"Oh my God!" Mami yelped as she walked into the room. She had come to assess the situation after she'd done her best to console his mom. "*Papi*, you're killing him! You're fucking

17

killing him! And you're shot, *papi*! Oh my god!" Mami screamed and tried to pull him off of Reggie.

Jahrome stood up and started to stomp him in the face. Blood coated his ankle socks, and he still didn't stop. He got dizzy and fell backward.

Mami led him into the bathroom and poured ice cold water on to his face, jolting him back to reality.

Babygirl had managed to slowly gained consciousness and muster up enough strength to crawled out of the room where she was met by her mother.

He sat up, and then jumped to his feet. "I'm finna kill this nigga! Don't nobody put their hands on my sister!" He started back toward the room when Mami pulled his arms, causing him to holler out in pain. "Arrgh! Shit!"

"*Papi*, we gotta get out of here. That nigga is dead. He's gone, *papi*. Hurry and look!" She said, leading him into the room.

Reggie was on his back with his eyes wide open. His face looked like it had been bashed in by a big ass brick. There was blood all over the room. Jahrome nodded. "That's what the fuck he gets."

He looked down and saw the four wrapped packages of heroin. "Where is my sister, Mami?"

Mami grabbed the gun off of the floor and put it into her bag. "Her and your mom took your car and hit it to the hospital. We gotta get out of here before the cops show up. I can't have yo' fine ass in prison. I'd hold you down, but that shit would kill me to the core."

Jahrome wrapped three bricks into the bed sheets, and took the other kilo, busting it open and pouring about half all over the room, before taping it closed with duct tape. "We gotta make this shit look like a robbery gone wrong or something, or else I'm just gonna dump this nigga's body in the river."

"Maybe you should-" Mami started to offer her suggestions, but Jahrome seemed to have had his mind made up.

"Matter of fact, that's what I'm finna do."

It took him ten minutes to wrap Reggie's body in five sheets. He took him out of the back door and loaded him into the trunk of his mother's old Buick, along with the two bricks he found beside his mother's house to use to tie around Reggie's ankles before tossing him into the river. After gathering all that he needed, him and Mami got in the car.

The car ride was uncomfortably silent. Both Mami and Jahrome were lost in their thoughts. Once they arrived at their destination, Jahrome remained quiet. It was as if he was in a trance.

He turned off the ignition and proceeded with the task at him. Without asking questions, Mami stepped out of the passenger side and assisted Jahrome in getting Reggie's body out of the trunk. Jahrome was caught off guard by Mami's willingness to help. After they were finished, she helped him back to the car.

Mami finally spoke."*Papi*, how are you feeling? Are you coming to my crib out in Marietta, Georgia? I need you to get down wit' my brother. He'll fuck wit' you on some hustle shit. You already know that dude Jock about to be at your head once he finds out about his brother."

Jahrome held his wounded shoulder. He thought about Jock and all of those niggas in Bankhead who ran under him. He knew that had Jock ever found out about him murdering Reggie, he would be forced to face pure hell. He respected Jock for being a pure goon. He feared for his mother and sister, more than his own life.

* * *

Jock waited until 3 a.m. before he pulled into the alley and parked the stolen Jeep Wrangler into the abandoned garage three houses down from Vick's house. Jock was a cocky dude at five foot nine inches tall weighing a solid 220 pounds. He had long dreads that flowed down his back just above his waist. His attitude was that of a person who didn't like be fucked with. He wasn't with the bullshit.

He was scheduled to meet with Toney-Wrong, an old school nigga who still had a little juice from back in the day when he was a street general. He'd just gotten back out from serving twenty years. While on lock, he held on to his juice, and niggas still honored him as a boss.

But since he had touched down, he was hollering a bunch of shit about cleaning up the neighborhood around Bankhead. He didn't want anyone hustling or selling pussy on his block. On top of that, he was trying to force Islam on everybody. Toney-Wrong was fucking up the game and making too much noise in his slums. Jock wasn't with that shit. The streets were his, and he was about to make sure it stayed that way.

A fat nigga named Biz opened the back door and nodded at Jock. "What's up, homie? Toney-Wrong is upstairs waiting on you." He closed the door. Before Jock could take the stairs, the guy said, "But before you go, I gotta pat you down. Rules are rules."

Jock mugged the fat nigga like he had lost his mind. "What you just say?"

Biz walked closer to the steps with his hand by his hip. He had already heard about Jock. The streets kept him in conversation. He didn't want any problems with the man. "Look, I'm just doing my job, man. I don't want no trouble

A Savage Dopeboy

out of you. I gotta search everybody because that's how shit goes around here."

Jock shook his head. "Homie, I'm letting you know right now that I'm strapped, just like you strapped, and I bet you any money that Toney-Wrong is strapped too. Now, I thought I could come to this muthafucking meeting without half of Bankhead up in this bitch, and you old niggas would respect my slot, but I see we're having a failure to communicate."

He reached into the back of his pants and pulled out two pistols: one 45, and one 9 millimeter Glock. He mugged Biz. "Nigga, what you gon' do?"

Biz's eyes were bugged out. Jock had the ups on him, and there was nothing he could do about it. "Say, Tony! Come get this crazy ass nigga, man! Hurry up before this muhfucka kills me!" Biz hollered.

Jock jumped off the steps and put the pistol to Biz's head. "You sound like a real bitch right now, my nigga. How 'bout you show some gangsta for the sake of yo' manhood?" He pressed the barrel to Biz's head hard, making his head lean backward. He was already unimpressed by the whole operation. He wondered how Toney-Wrong could have a soft nigga like Biz guarding the door. A man's security said a lot about his operation, and from what Jock was discovering, he was feeling like Toney-Wrong was just in the way even more.

"Whoa, whoa, whoa! Come on now, Jock. What the fuck you doing, son?" Toney-Wrong said with a .38 special in his hand walking into the room.

"Fuck this nigga. He trying to tell me that I can't have my security on me while I holler at you. That mean this bitch nigga expect for me to sit in front of you unprotected. That shit ain't happening." He turned over his shoulder and mugged Toney-Wrong. "You got a problem with that?"

The man shook his head, and took two steps back. "Naw, son. Those were my orders, so I'll take the blame for that. Give the brother a pass, my G." Jock mugged Biz for a long time before taking the pistol down.

"I'm gon' let you live this time, my nigga. But if you ever come at me bogus like that again, this old head gon' be having yo' funeral. Let's get this meeting under way." He walked into the house, bumping Toney-Wrong out of the way. Toney waited until he got inside before he looked at Biz, who still stood by the back door, steaming. Toney took his finger and slid it from one side of his neck to the other. Biz nodded and smiled.

Jock walked through the house, noting the smell of the calming Somali Rose incense. On the table in the dining room was about fifteen thousand dollars in cash, and a half of kilo of cocaine.

Jock frowned and shot Toney a dirty look. "Nigga, I thought you said you was trying to clean up the community? What the fuck is this?"

Toney smiled, stopped in front of his sound system, and turned on the Isley Brothers' "Groove with You." "Why don't you have a seat, little brother, so we can talk about the proposition I have for you?"

Jock sat down and placed both pistols on the table. He took a pinky nail and filled it with coke, tooting it hard up his left nostril. It gave him an instant feeling of euphoria, yet a dull high he couldn't enjoy for long. He was unimpressed. Toney sat down across from him, and offered him a shot of Crown Royal as he opened the bottle. He was trying to figure Jock out.

Jock held up his hand. "Fuck all this foreplay. What's good, my nigga? Why'd you call this meeting?"

Toney curled his upper lip. "I would prefer if you don't use that language in my presence. With that being said, this dope, and this money, is for you to leave Atlanta. I don't care where you go, or how far. I just want you out of this muhfucka, and fast."

Jock was already seeing red. That crazy Haitian in his blood came bubbling to the forefront. "What the fuck you just say to me about not doing in yo' muthafucking presence?" He stood up and grabbed both guns off of the table, aiming one at him, and the other at Biz, who had slowly made his way into the living room.

Toney mugged him, and Biz threw his hands in the air. "I told you calling this nigga over here was gon' be a bad idea. Everybody say he crazy. This young nigga ain't honoring shit."

Toney felt like Jock owed him respect because he had paved the way for him, and all of his niggas. He pointed to Jock's seat.

"Nigga, you betta sit yo' ass in that seat, and listen to what the fuck I gotta say. Don't you know I got O.G. status around here? You betta respect my slot. Now I want you out! O-U-T!"

Jock gave him a look like he was bored. "Really, my nigga?" He pulled out his gun, finger fucking the trigger. *Boom! Boom! Boom! Boom! Boom!*

He watched Toney fly backward with five big holes in his torso. Biz's fat ass tried to run, and he caught him in the back four times. *Boom! Boom! Boom! Boom!* Biz flew into the wall and slid down it slowly. He looked up to see Jock standing over him with an evil mug on his face.

"These my muthafucking streets. You niggas better get that shit through yo' head." *Boom! Boom! Boom! Boom!*

He stepped over Toney and saw that he was still struggling to breathe. He knelt down and put the .45 to his forehead and pulled the trigger. *Boom!* The back of his head opened up and shot pieces of his brains out.

Jock looked down on him and shook his head in disgust. He vowed to never wind up like the old nigga. He promised that when the game told him his time was up, he would be more than ready to depart from it with a whole lot of money.

He snatched up the money and dope from the table. He ransacked the whole house and came up with another thirty thousand dollars. In his mind, the meeting had been a success.

Chapter 3

Jahrome woke up the next morning writhing in pain. Mami had finally convinced him to the emergency room where they patched up his shoulder wound, after taking the round out of him. He had refused the pain medication and was paying for it at that moment.

The nurses had been slick enough to slip out of his room and act as if they were going to get his release forms. A police officer had shown up to take his statement in regards to his gunshot wound.

"Sir, my name is Officer John McNaulty." He extended his hand for Jahrome to shake, but yet again he was refusing to speak. "Sir, I know you're probably not in the mood to talk to me, but I cannot assist you if I do not know what happened."

"I didn't ask fo' yo' muthfuckin' assistance. You ain't here to help shit. You don't give a fuck about me. All you pigs look to do is lock a black ma'fucka up." Jahrome had grew quite irritated with Officer McNaulty pretending like he gave a fuck. He was far from stupid.

"Sir, I can understand your frustrations, but I kindly ask you to refrain from the name calling and hostility. Can you please tell me how you obtain that gunshot wound to your shoulder?"

Jahrome gave him the cold shoulder and kept silence.

"Here's my card. When you are ready to speak, give me a call. If I do not hear from you soon, I will come looking for you." Officer McNaulty left in peace but made it his business to be on alert.

Jahrome was thankful the gun Reggie used to shoot him was also in the river with him. After finally being cleared to leave the emergency room, him and Mami headed home.

Mami didn't know what was going on with him so she thought it'd be best to leave well enough alone.

Mami came out of the kitchen and sat on the bed next to him with a tray of food. "Buenos días, *papi*. How are you feeling this morning?" She kissed him on the cheek and nuzzled her face into his neck. His scent drove her crazy. Everything about him was intoxicating, even his bloody gauze.

Jahrome tried to move his shoulder, and the pain shot up his body. "Yo, I'm fucked up. This pain is killing me right now, ma." He closed his eyes tight and bit into his bottom lip.

Mami was willing to do anything to make him feel better. She felt like it was her job to protect him. "Do you want some head, *papi*? Maybe it'll take your mind away from the pain for a little while." She stood up, and sat the tray on the dresser.

Jahrome noticed she had on some pink , laced Victoria Secret boy shorts that were all up in her round ass. As she took a step, her ass cheeks jiggled along with her thick thighs. As bad as the pain was in his shoulder, the pain in his dick was starting to overpower it.

He looked around the room. "Mami, I thought you said your brother lived here too. Where that nigga at?" Every time he got to pounding Mami, she'd scream at the top of her lungs. The fit between her thighs was snug, and his dick was a lot to handle.

He didn't want to be laying pipe on her and Rico show up on some bullshit. He'd only met the nigga once, and he couldn't really place his temperament.

Mami looked at him over her shoulder, and popped back on her legs, making her ass jiggle. She was slightly bowlegged, and her long curly brown hair all over her face was doing something to him.

She sucked her bottom lip, and slowly walked back over to the bed. "He's in East Atlanta right now. He spent a night over his baby mother's house, and from what she said, he was fucked up off of that Jose Cuervo, so I ain't expecting to see that fool until sometime this afternoon. So no worries, *papi*. We're good. Just let me do what I do."

She ran her tongue across her lips. Her nipples were already poking through her small wife beater. She knelt down and massaged his dick through his boxers until she felt his log rising. As soon as she felt it, she pulled it through his boxer hole, stroking it up and down. It stood up like a mini baseball bat. She loved the sight of it, didn't waste any time sucking it.

Jahrome's eyes rolled into the back of his head. He tried so hard to enjoy this moment and to let go of the pain he was facing; the pain of his sister being in the hospital, the pain of losing his mother's respect for not being there, and the pain in his shoulder. He wanted to release them all, but just couldn't

Mami sucked up and down his pole, moaning all the while. Her thick lips were working overtime. In her mind, there was nothing like a big, black dick. It made her feel like she was dealing with a powerful and strong man. She couldn't help but be submissive.

She stroked it a few times, then stood up. She slid her wife beater over her head, exposing her brown beauties. Her nipples were incredibly hard. She took her hands and squeezed her breasts together, rolling the long nipples in her finger before pulling them.

"*Papi*, I know you're hurt right now, but after watching how you got down yesterday, I need you to fuck me. *Por favor*, I just need you inside of me, and I'll do anything you want afterwards. Please, *papi*." She took two fingers and started rubbing them up and down the slit in her tight panties. It didn't take long before the cloth was soaking wet.

Jahrome was in a trance watching her. He tried his best to clear his mind and make it all about her. He stroked his dick up and down, taking in her sexy ass body. "Get yo' ass up here and ride this dick, then. Don't get on me if you gon' play wit' my pipe though. I'm gon' push yo' ass off me."

Mami moaned deeply. She loved how he talked to her. She was so used to men bowing down at her feet. Jahrome was the only man who didn't give a fuck. He talked that thug shit to her that drove her crazy. It made her want to bow down to his gangsta at all times.

Jahrome watched her slide her panties off. Her pussy was fat as a peach and her lips were engorged. She spread her legs and slid two fingers in her box, sliding them in and out, before sucking her own juices off of them.

"Get yo' ass up here, man." Jahrome demanded. He needed to be inside her.

She quickly got on the bed and straddled him. Jahrome held his dick, sliding it up and down her lips, until the head sunk in, then he pulled her down by her hips, and she yelped loudly in pleasurable pain.

"Uhhnnn, sssss, *papi*. Yesssss!" She opened her mouth and threw her head back. Jahrome felt her hotness gripping his dick, and slammed her down on him hard, forcing her to rise and fall again. Her breasts jiggled to his rhythm.

He squeezed them together before sucking on the nipples hard while she bounced up and down in his lap wildly, moaning like crazy.

"Unnn, *papi*! Yes, *papi*! Fuck this Rican pussy! Fuck this Rican pussy with that big dick, *papi*! Please! Fuck meeee!" She screamed, cumming in short jerks, while he slobbered over her big titties.

The pussy was hot and wet, and the scent in the air made it that much better. He flipped her over and wrapped his hand around her neck, throwing her thick thighs on to his shoulder. He thrusted into her, and choked her a little bit, while fucking that pussy hard.

"This my muthafucking pussy. Tell daddy you love this shit! Tell me you love the way I'm beating these walls in. Tell me!" He leaned forward, stroking with so much force she could barely talk. Her walls held on to him for dear life, and only made him beat it harder.

"*Te amo, papi! Te amo, papi!* I love it! I love it! Ohhhh, shit, I love it sooo much!" She felt him wrecking her kitty, and the harder he piped her down, the stronger she fell for him. It ended with her laying on her stomach, and him sucking all over her thick ass cheeks, while she cried in his arms.

It was the norm for her to cry afterwards. There was just something about him that drove her mad. She felt him smack her on the ass hard and suck it again.

For him, there was nothing like a big ass booty. He felt women with fat asses deserved to have them worshipped.

* * *

Babygirl stirred from her slumber as felt kisses against her forehead. She opened her eyes slowly until her brother's handsome face came into view. Jahrome looked concerned, yet angry at the same time. He leaned in and kissed her on the cheek. His mother sat across from her, not even acknowledging him.

"Hey, lil' momma. How are you doing?" He blinked and a tear slid down his cheek.

Babygirl swallowed, and tried to sit up, before he held her shoulder, preventing her. "Nah, ma, just chill. I don't want you moving unless you absolutely have to." He grabbed her hand

and kissed it. They still had her hooked up to an I.V. He was told that she was doing okay, with the exception of her face.

Babygirl smiled. "I knew you would come for me, Jahrome. I knew you wasn't gon' let me stay in this hospital unprotected. You've always protected me ever since we were kids." She reached up and pulled his head down so she could kiss him on the cheek. Tears fell out of her eyes. "The doctor told me he scarred up my face pretty bad. He said I ain't never gon' be pretty no more." She whimpered.

"He didn't say that." Linda spoke up.

"He might as well have, momma. He said the scar will be there for the rest of my life. That means I will never be pretty again. How am I gon' make a living? Don't nobody want no ugly stripper in their lap, and I sho' can't be a main attraction anymore. My life is ruined, and all for what?" She started crying, and tried to turn on to her side, before Jahrome stopped her.

Jahrome looked over his shoulder at Mami and his mother. "Yo, let me have the room real fast. I gotta holla at her on some private talk."

Linda frowned. "Boy, we're family. We don't keep secrets from each other. Anything you gotta say to her you can say in front of me."

Jahrome smiled warmly. He had a deep respect for his mother, and would never step outside of that. "Momma, please. I'm asking you for this one favor."

Mami rubbed Linda's back. "Come on, Ms Linda, let's just give them a little privacy. We'll come back in five minutes or so."

Linda eyed him closely. "Well, alright. But I don't like this family keeping secrets and all that shit. We're all we have." She lowered her head as Mami led her out into the hallway.

"How about we go get you something to eat? How does that sound?"

"Sounds good, baby."

As soon as they were out of the room, Jahrome got up and closed the door. He rubbed his sister's cheek with his thumb. He slowly started to peel back the huge Band-Aid across her face.

"Lil' bro, what are you doing?" Babygirl asked, holding her head steady.

Jahrome blinked back tears. "Be cool, man. I just wanna see what this bitch ass nigga did to you." He continued until he pulled it away, exposing the deep gash. He was speechless.

Reggie had screwed his sister's face up. Babygirl was extremely gorgeous, and Reggie knew that, so he made it his business to try and scar her for life, and he'd succeeded. Babygirl sat back in the bed with her eyes on the ceiling.

"It's that bad, huh?" Tears ran from her eyes, and into her ears. Jahrome bounced back up and leaned down, brushing her hair away from her forehead. He took a deep breath and brought his lips right on to her wound. It was still slightly bleeding, but he didn't care. The stitches felt rough against his lips.

Babygirl was his heart, the only person in the world who understood him, and would ride for him under any and all circumstances. They'd had a rough childhood growing up and had been through so much together.

Her wound only made him love her even more. He wanted her to know and understand how beautiful she was regardless.

"I swear on our mother you're still the most beautiful woman in the world. Ain't nobody got shit on you, Babygirl. Do you hear me?"

You are the truth, ma, and I'll kill any ma'fucka who says you ain't. That's my word." He felt his heart beating faster before he placed the huge bandage back over her wound.

"I'm glad you think so, Jahrome, because I'm going to need your strength. I don't know what I'm gon' do with myself. I don't know how I'm gon' eat, and I don't know how I'm gon' pay my portion of the rent for a while. They ain't gone fuck wit' me in that club. You already know that. There's plenty of bad bitches jocking for my slot. What am I gon' do? I damn sure can't depend on Reggie, but after this, he probably the only nigga who gon' want me." She sighed in defeat.

Jahrome shot her a mean look. Her eyes got wide. "What? I'm just kidding. I'll never fuck wit' that nigga again. That's on our mom."

Jahrome curled his upper lip as a slight devilish smile cept across his face. "That fuck nigga dead anyway." He rubbed her forehead with his thumb.

Babygirl felt like she wanted to throw up. Her eyes bucked. She wasn't sure she fully understood. *No, he did not*, she thought . If he had killed Reggie, then that meant they weren't safe. His brother, Jock, would come for them, or even worse, it meant Jahrome could go to prison.

Babygirl tried her best to breathe. "What do you mean he's dead?" She asked calmly.

Jahrome frowned. "Look, when I ran in there, that fool was messing you up, sis, and I snapped. You already know how crazy I am over you. I told you if any nigga ever put their hands on you again after what Pops did, I was gon' body their ass with no hesitation. My word is my bond, and you are my heart. I'd kill a million niggas over you."

He knelt down and laid his head on her chest, while she traced his deep waves with her fingers. Their father had been an extremely abusive man all throughout their childhood.

32

Often times, coming home in a drunken stupor, he'd beat them for no reason. His blows used to send Babygirl to the hospital on a regular basis.

Babygirl thought back on all of that chaos, and how a young Jahrome used to stand toe-to-toe with the man, three years younger than her, but still fighting to protect her. It made her heart melt. She knew without a shadow of a doubt he would do anything for her.

He stood up and exhaled. "Now, I know when that nigga T puts two and two together, word gon' get back to Jock, and he'll be here to see me." He curled his upper lip. "So what I'm finna do is get my weight up and go see that nigga first. I think I gotta body T, too, just to cover all bases."

Babygirl sat up. Although, she was worried, she trusted her brother. He'd always proven himself trustworthy. She motioned for him to come to her. She waited until he was standing in front of her, and then she wrapped her arms around him, pressing her face against his chest. "I love you so much, Jahrome, and I already know you 'bout that life. I just want you to be careful, and I need for you to be smart because I need you more than ever. In this world, I know you're the only one who truly loves me, outside of our mom. You're my everything."

Jahrome nodded, and knew it was in his best interest to figure things out because it wouldn't be long before them Bankhead niggas would be on his heels.

Chapter 4

Jock had a two story, red-brick home over in Buckhead that he considered his duck off. It was where his baby mother and his 9-year-old daughter stayed, and he made sure that it was decked out from the basement to the attic. His baby mother's name was Dymond, and she was all about her paper.

Before she'd gotten pregnant, she was just one of the hood chicks he fucked around with growing up, the ones who were so strapped that every nigga in the hood be trying to fuck them. She was skinny up top, but her thighs and ass were enticing.

They went to Malcolm X Middle School together, and graduated. By the time they made it to Rufus King High, Jock was sneaking through her bedroom window, eating her pussy and trying to get her ready for sex because she was always saying she was scared.

One day, he had gotten her to smoke half of a blunt with him, and she got real freaky. Usually, when he laid her on the bed, he could tell she was getting nervous. This time, when he laid her back and pulled her skirt up, she didn't say anything. She only bit into her bottom lip as he rubbed her little pussy through her tight panties.

"Ummm, Jock, stop that. Here you go being nasty again. You know my momma gon' be home in a little while. You gotta go." She moaned.

Jock wasn't hearing any of that. He sniffed her box, and her scent caused him to get rock hard. Moving her panties to the side, he sucked her left lip, and pulled back the right, exposing her strawberry-colored center.

"Ummmm, shit! What are you doing, baby?" She cried, closing her eyes tight. The feeling was driving her crazy. She opened her legs wider, slding her hand under her bra, playing with her big nipples. "Unnnn! "

Jock slurped her lips into his mouth while his thumb ran back and forth across her clitoris. She humped into his face, and that made him grip her ass, squeezing it. He buried his face into her more deeply, and flicked his tongue over her clit.

The feeling became intense. Her breathing quickened. What he was doing to her was the only thing that mattered. It was sending her on a journey she could not understand. When he got to talking to her like a savage, it was just too much. She heard herself screaming, before the intense shaking started. "Uhhhhhhhhh, shiiiit! I'm cummming!"

Jock sucked harder and rubbed her clit harder with his thumb. "Come for me, baby. Come all on my lips. Ummm-arrrghh!" He went crazy with his face going from side to side. He knew that he had did his job. He waited for her to stop shaking before he stood up with his dick out.

"Come on, man, you already know the drill."

The norm was for her to open her legs while he looked at her play with her fat pussy. She would often close her eyes because she was so shy, but this day, she had something different written all over her face. He could tell that she was ready.

"Jock, if you promise you won't hurt me, and you'll just do it a little bit, you can have it. " She bit into her lower lip, and rubbed her big thighs together. Her skin was caramel colored, but when you got to her inner thighs, her skin was darker, almost the shade of black, and it drove him crazy.

Jock damn near broke. "Alright, that's cool, but you gotta do it my way, and listen to me. That way, it won't hurt so much for your first time."

Dymond nodded. "What do you want me to do?" She squeezed her thighs together and could feel her clit tingling.

"Come here and bend over, because that's the easiest way. Just trust me."

Dymond nervously got out of the bed and bent over in front of him. She was ready, but anxious about losing her virginity. She felt him rubbing all over her ass. She felt like a slut, but in a good way. When his fingers found her wet gap, she spread her legs wider and moaned.

"Pull yo' titties out, baby, and look at yourself in that mirror. You all mines tonight."

Dymond pulled her shirt up and off, then unhooked her bra from the front, allowing her titties to spill out. She felt him reach around and squeeze them, and it drove her crazy. She always liked when boys played with her breasts. Jock rubbed his dick head up and down her slippery gap until the head slipped into her hole a little bit, then he grabbed her hips.

"Alright, shawty, here it go. You said go slow, right?"

She moaned, "Yeah because I don't want it to hurrrrt!"

She yelped out in pain as he entered her and began slow stroking her, but less than five minutes into it, she was throwing her ass back at him, begging him to murder her coochie. He grabbed her hips and went to work. He saw the small traces of blood run down her thighs before it was replaced by her juices.

That first time had cost them so much trouble, because not only had her mother caught them and kicked her out of the house at 14, she had gotten pregnant with their daughter, and he'd been out grinding for their family ever since.

He shook his head at the old memories as he stepped through the door of his home, and dropped the pillowcase filled with money and dope on the floor.

Dymond came from the kitchen with a big cake bowl in her hand, whipping the batter, with her cell phone stuck to her ear, head leaned to the side.

She walked up to him and kissed him on the lips. "Hey, baby, how are you feeling?" She eyed the pillowcase and already knew he had been out on business.

Jock took off his black T-shirt, and unsnapped his bulletproof vest, dropping it on the floor, revealing a hard body of muscles and tattoos. "I got three kilos of heroin. I need you to bust that shit down and get it ready for me to take to the traps after I get out the shower. There's also a few bands. I want you to get my daughter them red bottoms she been bugging me about. Get her three pairs in different colors, and you get whatever you want too, matter of fact." He knelt down and went into the bag, pulling out the cash and counting off fifteen G's.

Dymond hung the phone up and threw it on the couch. Grabbing the money, she licked her thumb, and counted it quickly. "I need me a new bag, too. T just bought Star a new Birkin, and that bitch won't shut up about it."

Jock waved her off. "You know I don't get into all that shit. It's my job to keep you in top-of-the-line everything, so if you feeling like that bitch flexing on you, then do yo' thing. That's yo' right as my wiz." She smiled and wrapped her arms around his neck, kissing his chocolate skin.

"You know I love you, right?" She was literally nuts about her man, and had been ever since they were kids. They'd been trapping on the streets together ever since they were teens.

Jock had been finding dope boys as ways to make ends meet, and he had done a damn good job of it. She not only loved his violent and crazy ass, she trusted him.

She stood on her tiptoes, and kissed him on the cheek. "I love you, baby."

Jock released her. He didn't really feel like being on some lovey-dovey shit. He had so many things on his mind that he needed to get in order. Being emotional was at the bottom of his list. "Yeah, shorty, I love yo' ass, too. Now get a nigga something to eat. I'm hungry as a muthafucka." He walked over, and plopped on the couch. He yawned and closed his eyes.

Dymond popped back on her legs and laughed. "Yeah, alright. Is there anything in general you want?"

Jock shook his head. "Just food. Something fried."

She nodded. "Hey, have you heard from your brother Reggie lately?"

Jock yawned again and got comfortable on the couch. "Why you asking me that?"

"Because T called looking for him. Shit, everybody been looking for him. He been M.I.A. for a few days now."

She picked up her phone and saw a text from Star, saying they just found Reggie's body. Dymond dropped the phone and screamed. "Oh my God! Oh my God!"

Jock rises from the couch, pulling two Desert Eagles from his holsters. "Bitch, what the fuck is you screaming for?" He snapped.

Dymond pointed to her phone on the ground. "They just found Reggie's body, baby. He's dead."

Ghost

Chapter 5

It was ninety degrees in Atlanta. Jock stood back a safe distance, as Reggie's body was being exhumed from the swamp. He clenched his teeth in anger. He couldn't imagine who would have enough heart to come at his little brother. Everybody in Atlanta knew who Reggie's older brother was. They knew Jock was a beast. Most had heard many horrific stories about him. Stories that were true and gruesome. He shook his head, white hot with fury.

There was a crowd of eighty people being nosey. They were recording the event with their cellphones. This made Jock even madder. He hated nosey people, and he hated the fact that there was so many of them around. He wanted to get to the bottom of what had taken place, but he wasn't going to depend on the law's investigation. In Bankhead, things were handled on street terms. It was plain and simple.

Jock looked across the way and saw Reggie's body being laid on the grass. The police took pictures of him, and placed markers all around him, before pulling a black sheet over his remains. One thing Jock had been able to see before his brother had been covered was the fact that his skull appeared to have been smashed inward. This caused Jock to become even more furious.

He saw Dymond speaking with one of the investigators. She kept nodding her head. After shaking hands with the investigator, she made her way over to him, just as Star appeared out of the crowd. Star placed her arm around Dymond's neck and walked with her to Jock.

Jock grabbed Dymond by the wrist and brought her aggressively to his Range Rover. He opened the door and ordered her to get inside of it. "Get yo' ass in and let me holler at you for a minute."

Dymond frowned but followed his commands. She slammed the door and crossed her arms in front of her chest. She looked at Star, who pursed her lips and shook her head slowly. She seemed to be taking pity on her. This irritated Dymond.

Jock got into the truck and slammed his door. He mugged Star for a second until she turned her back on him and walked back into the crowd. He turned on his air conditioner and shifted the vents, so the cool air was blowing on his face. "Fuck was dude hollering at you about?"

Dymond was silent for a moment. "Why you always gotta snatch me up and shit, Jock? Why you just couldn't tell me to sit down in your truck so we could holler?" She was tired of him treating her as if she were nothing more than his maid and rag doll. She did genuinely love him. He was her first, but she felt that she deserved some respect after all they had been through together.

"Bitch, I ain't tryna hear none of that shit. You my woman. If I wanna snatch yo' ass up every single day for the rest of our lives, then that's what I'ma do. Stop asking me all of these stupid ass questions and answer my question. Now what the fuck happened to my brother?" He spat.

Dymond sighed. "They really can't say until they have the full autopsy report. But just by first glance, it looks as if his head was beat in with a blunt object. I don't know who could've done something like that to him. Do you?"

Jock mugged his brother's covered body. "Hell, naw, I don't know who did that shit to him. But I'ma find out. And until I find out who did this shit, I'ma fuck this city over. I ain't finna leave no stone unturned over my brother."

"That's understandable. Reggie was a good man. He loved you, and he looked up to you a lot. I don't know who could've possibly did this to him, but one thing is for sure, they aren't going to get away with it. I feel sorry for them."

Jock flared his nostrils. "Naw, shorty, don't feel sorry for them fuck niggas. They should've factored all of this shit in before they made a move on my blood. Now mafuckas finna feel the wrath of an animal. That's on Bankhead."

His eyes scanned the crowd until they rested on T. T was fitted in a black and gray Red Monkey outfit with matching Airmax shoes. He had three gold ropes around his neck that were blinging with ice.

Jock rolled down his window and yelled, "Say, T! Say, let me holler at you for a minute, mane."

When T saw Jock, he cursed under his breath. He hugged Star, and made his way through the crowd to Jock's black-on-black Range Rover. "What it do, playboy?" He hollered past Dymond.

Jock laid back and rested both .40 Glocks on his lap. He mugged T. "Nigga, we got a muthafuckin' problem."

T felt the sweat bead down the side of his face. He wiped it away and shielded his eyes from the sun. "Potna, I already know this shit is fucked up right here, but you best believe that I'm finna get to the bottom of this."

Jock ran his tongue across his teeth. "Yeah, all that shit sound sweeter than high fructose corn syrup, but it ain't doing shit to appease the fire in my brain right now. So you finna hop yo' ass in and we finna take a spin."

T waved him off. "No can do right now. I got some shit I need to take care of, but I can fuck wit' you a lil' later on tonight, if you're able."

Jock sat up and mugged him. "Nigga, what the fuck you just say?"

T scoffed and shielded his eyes from the sun again. "You heard me, bruh. Now, I understand this shit is fucked up, but at the same time, I gotta handle my side of things. That's just the way the game go." He looked Jock in the eyes. He could tell that he was getting irritated, but he didn't care. He disliked the way the man spoke down to him.

Jock smiled and looked past T's shoulder to the group of police officers who weren't that far away. He had visions on blasting him right where he stood outside of his truck, but he knew the cops would have moved in on him immediately. It would have been a pure suicide mission.

"Check this out, homeboy. I don't give a fuck what you talking about. My brother laying over there dead on the pavement, and you standing around this muthafucka still alive. You finna tell me something, or I'm finna put yo' ass at the top of my to-do list. Now fuck wit' me, potna."

T grunted and laughed to himself. "That's how you feel, Jock?"

Jock, glanced over T's shoulder again. "Nigga, it's in yo' best interest to not play wit' me. Jump in this ma'fucka so we can get an understanding."

He reached across Dymond and opened the door. "Bitch, get yo' ass out and go and fuck wit' Star. I need to holler at the homie for a minute."

Dymond mugged him and grabbed her Hermes bag. She got out without looking back. He made her so mad. She hated how he had no problem disrespecting her in front of other people.

"Dymond, don't take yo' monkey ass too far. All I'm finna do is take a spin around a few blocks, and I'ma be right back."

Dymond waved him off and kept right on walking until she met up with Star.

Star saw her and grabbed both of her shoulders. "Girl, what's wrong with you? Are you okay?"

44

Dymond blinked tears. "I'm just so tired of him. I'm tired of all of this bullshit. Where is your car? We need to take a drive."

Star nodded in understanding. "Okay, that's cool. I'ma send T a text and let him know what's good, and we'll go from there."

***

Jock pulled away from the curb and looked over at T. "Nigga, tell me why you're still alive, and my lil' brother is back there stanking?"

Every time Jock looked T over, he knew something wasn't right. He had on way too much jewelry, and it gave Jock the wrong vibe. He wondered if he had robbed and killed his brother. .

"Look, I don't know what happened to him, but like I said, I'ma get to the bottom of it. That was my nigga." T surveyed the streets as they rolled down them.

Jock was surveying the same way. He was a natural-born hunter. "My brother had some of my work, a few bricks that he was getting ready to move for me. Can you tell me where my shit is now?"

T continued to scan the blocks they rolled down, looking for potential enemies or threats. He didn't see anything suspicious. "Whatever bruh had going on with you ain't my business. He was his own man. All I can say is that knowing him, he would have more than likely busted that work down with me, and I would've made sure we pushed that shit day and night until it was gone. I'm bout that paper, Jock, but you already know that." T adjusted his chains, and smiled, before turning it into a quick frown.

Jock wanted to spit in his face. He never liked T. He felt that T thought he was too hard for his own good. He also didn't trust him. And any man he didn't trust was considered a threat. "Mane, I can't put my mafuckin' finger on what's going on just yet, but you betta hope I never find out you had anything to do wit' my brother's murder, 'cause if I do, we gon' have a serious problem."

Jock pulled into a gas station, in front of one of the gas pumps. He pulled out a fifty dollar bill. "Bruh, go in there and put forty on my tank for me." He handed the bill to T.

T grabbed it from him and wanted to curse his ass out for treating him like a worker instead of an up and coming boss. But instead of arguing with Jock, he grabbed the money, and jumped out of the whip.

As he headed inside, he read the latest text from Star saying Dymond would be spending the night at their place. He began to text back asking why. The last thing he wanted to do was to put up with Jock's bitch.

Jock opened the glove compartment to place his glasses back inside of it, when his .9 millimeter fell out of it and hit the floor. He leaned over to pick it up, when a masked enemy rolled up on a ten-speed bicycle and hopped off of it. He took the .38 Special off of his hip and aimed at Jock's driver side window. "Say, bitch nigga, fuck Bankhead!" *Boom! Boom! Boom! Boom!*

The glass to Jock's window exploded. The gunman saw Jock leaning on the passenger's door. He ran around and fired two more shots to the other side. He yanked open the door, aimed his gun at Jock's face, and pulled the trigger four times. *Click! Click! Click! Click!* Seeing his gun was empty, he took off running, leaving his bike behind him.

T flew out of the store, running full speed behind the hitta with his Glock in his left hand. The gunmen turned into an alley and picked up speed. He threw garbage cans behind him as he ran and tried knock T off of his path. T stopped in the center of the filthy alley and fired.

Bocka! Bocka! Bocka! His fourth bullet zipped, and closed the distance between the two, before it slammed into the gunman's back and knocked him off of his feet. He hollered out in pain and struggled to get up. T closed the distance swiftly. He stood over the gunman. "Snake ass nigga!" *Bocka! Bocka! Bocka!*

Ghost

Chapter 6

Mami watched Jahrome pace back and forth in her living room. They were watching the news, and it showed the authorities pulling Reggie's body out of the river.

Jahrome kept on shaking his head in panic. "Fuck, I'm finna have to holla at this nigga already. I know how them Bankhead niggas get down. Once he finds out I bodied his brother, the shit finna hit the fan." He said, trying to calm down.

He felt like going over there and sweating Jock before he could even come at him. He believed the worst thing he could do was wait for the enemy to attack. That was basically suicide.

Mami stood up, walked over, and started rubbing his back. "*Papi*, calm down, and fuck them niggas. They bleed just like you do. If they think it's sweet, then you just gon' have to show their asses. That's why I want you to get down with my brother."

Then, the whole house felt like it was shaking. She ran over and looked out the window. They heard Daddy Yankee's "Gasolina" blasting outside.

Mami jumped up and down in excitement. "That's him, baby! That's him!" She opened the door, and her brother turned off the music.

Rico stepped into the doorway and picked her up, wrapping his arms around her. "Hey, little sister! How are you, *mamita*?" He kissed her on the cheek.

"I'm doing good, but my man ain't. I need for you to put him down with you ASAP, Rico. Muhfuckas think they about to hurt him, and it ain't even going down like that." She frowned her face and pointed at Jahrome. "Go! Handle yo' business."

Rico pinched his nose and smiled. "You're just like our mother, always giving me orders and shit." He nodded when he walked toward Jahrome. "What's up wit' you, homie? You need heat, or what?"

Jahrome didn't know how to respond. He wasn't the type of nigga to bow down to anybody.

Mami stepped in. "Look, that fool, Reggie, was trying to get at me the other day, and he tried to rape me. My man stepped in and killed his ass. Simple as that. Now, we're worried about Reggie's brother over there in Bankhead finding out and bringing the drama our way. After all, he was defending my honor." She lied.

Rico felt his temper run hot. "Some muthafucker tried to rape you, sis, and you ain't tell me shit? What kind of crap is that, Mami?" He asked with an evil look on his face.

Mami stood behind Jahrome. "It was taken care of, Rico. That's the only reason why. He reacted right away and handled his business. Why you tripping, *hermano*?"

Rico nodded. "I'm about to go shut that muthafucker down, Mami. Nobody fucks with my *hermana*. *Sabes que* nobody fucks with the king or the Kings' family."

He turned to head out of the door, but Mami grabbed his arm. "Rico, wait! Please, just hear me out." She grabbed him and hugged him. "Those fools know where his family lives, so if you make any mistakes, they're going to wipe them out, and that ain't cool. Why don't you just plug him into your Kings, and when it's time to go to war, have his back like he had mine? Besides, he gotta eat, and you need a goon like him on your squad."

Rico looked at her for a long time, then he looked over Jahrome closely. He usually didn't fuck with niggas on that level, but the man had saved his sister's life, so he felt indebted to him.

"Where I'm from, we squeeze hammers to eat, and ain't nobody in my crew show mercy. Now, I appreciate what you did for my sister, but I don't give no handouts. If you fucking with me and living in my jungle, you gon' eat like a muthafucking lion. Everybody prey, even bitches. That's just the way it is because it's all about the money at the end of the day. We're warring with the Clayton Cobras right now, and them muthafuckas don't play either, so if you're down with me, you're killing them niggas off every day, but in exchange, you gone have some hitters with you, and whenever you feel like you're ready to fuck over them Bankhead fools, then there's no mercy. Deal?" He extended his hand.

Jahrome shook it, and nodded his head. "I ain't into handouts either, my nigga, and I'm riding for any muthafucka who's riding for me. My loyalty is one hunnit."

Rico nodded, went into his back pocket, and handed Jahrome a brand new .45, all chrome. "This is yours right here. Tonight, I'll pick you up for your initiation."

* * *

Later that night, Rico came over. Mami hopped up from Jahrome's lap and answered it. He hugged her, then walked over to Jahrome and handed him a MAC-10.

"You fucking wit' me solo tonight. I got the drop on one of these Cobra niggas who's doing a deal with some of the Asian Bloods. We don't fuck with them either, but the fools we're hitting tonight shot up a few of the homies, and kilt a fifteen-year-old girl about a month ago. Names aren't important, but I gotta see how you get down before I introduce you to the rest of the mob. You handle yo' business, and you're in. Trust me on that."

Jahrome didn't care who he was killing. He needed the Rican's backup whenever shit kicked off with Jock. "I'm wit' it, my nigga. Let's roll out."

"Wait!" Mami said, jumping up from the couch. She leaned over and picked up a candle, lighting it. As soon as it was lit, she did the sign of the crucifix over her brother first, and then Jahrome.

"Holy Mary, mother of God, please protect these men. Bless and protect these men." She said the last statement two more times, then kissed the both of them on each cheek.

Rico walked out of the house first, and Mami pulled Jahrome by the arm. "Please be careful, *papi*. I need you, and I want you to know I love you. My brother is very crazy. He doesn't fear death. He welcomes it with open arms. You have to watch yourself because if you don't, you'll be hurt severely. Now, when you get back here, your sister will be here. She says that she can't be away from you, and I okayed her to come over." She kissed him on the lips with her eyes closed.

A few moments later, he was sitting in the passenger's seat of Rico's 2018 all-black Durango. It had all-yellow leather interior. He had TVs in every head rest, and they were also in his steering wheel. The car smelled like heavy loud-pack.

"My sister has never blessed any man along side of me. She must really care about you, which is odd, because you kinda sprung up out of nowhere. What gives?"

Jahrome thought about what Mami said about Rico welcoming death, and while he wasn't afraid of it, he wasn't in a rush to get to it. He didn't want to talk about the feelings Mami had for him. "There should be plenty time to talk about all of that later. For now, I need you to let me know what we're about to do."

Rico took the fat blunt out of the ashtray and lit it, took two strong pulls, and handed it to Jahrome. "This here is directly from the mother land. Grown right in my grandparents' backyard. We got the seeds from the caves of El Morro. Try it."

Jahrome held the heavy blunt in his hand, and took a strong pull. He blew a cloud, and sucked it back into his mouth, holding it, feeling the burn. He took another pull before he blew that one out and did the same thing. He slowly felt himself becoming high as a kite. He handed the blunt back to Rico.

"There should be about eight niggas present. We gotta body everyone we see, because if we don't, and one of them fools make it, trust me, they'll be back. There's gonna be a party going on downstairs in the basement. The deal is going on upstairs. I got a bitch who's gon' let us in. She's down with the crew, and she's authentic, so don't worry about her. When she lets us in, we gotta get up those stairs fast, and handle business. I'll split everything with you, and Friday, I'll introduce you to the family at our gold meeting."

Jahrome felt a little uneasy because he had never gotten down with the man before. He didn't know how he did his thing with the hammers, so that made him nervous. Then, he heard Mami's voice reassuring him. If it came down to it, he had to make sure he did whatever he had to do to make it out of their situation alive. It was all about self-preservation.

* * *

T should have known there was going to be some bullshit involved when Jock called him in the middle of the night and told him to meet him at "the spot" in the projects. When he asked him what for, he simply told him that he would find out when he got there. But common sense told him that it had something to do with Reggie.

Jock took the thin, green straw and tooted up the cocaine from the small saucer, before pinching his nostrils and tooting another line. He was sitting at the table with T. After that one, he took a swallow from the bottle of Ace of Spades. "Only a few muhfuckas knew about them bricks I gave my little brother. You, and my nigga, Spook, because he was there when I gave them to him, and me. Shit ain't making sense, my nigga, so I need you to fill me in."

Jock still couldn't understand how the man had wound up in the river. He tried to play over every scenario in his head, and nothing was making sense. They hadn't been in any drama with anybody he could think of who would body him like that.

Jock tooted another line, took his .40 Glock off of his waist, and set it on the table with the barrel pointed toward T. "I appreciate how you handled business the other day on that nigga who tried to body me, but I'm not fully convinced, my nigga. You were my brother's right-hand man. Now, he's dead, and you sitting here untouched. I need for you to make shit make sense for me."

T took a deep breath and sat back in his chair. "Last time I talked to him was last Friday night. We all played dominos and kicked it a lil' bit. When I left, bruh was good. He said he was gon' holla at his woman about some shit that was disrespectful to him, I guess, but nonetheless, he was still breathing."

Jock took the .40 and cocked it, then set it back on the table. He took a swallow from the bottle of Ace and directed the barrel of the gun at T again. "Who was all there?"

T felt the sweat pour down his neck onto his back. He fidgeted in his chair. "Bruh, you gotta point the gun at me like that?" He asked, feeling a little disrespected. He knew Jock was running the show, but at the same time, he didn't feel he should have been coming at him like this.

T and Reggie had grown up together, and they were basically inseparable. There had never been any shadiness between them. He always looked to Jock as if he were an older brother, and he couldn't understand why he was getting down on him.

Jock took another long swallow and set the bottle on the table calmly. He nodded. "That's a good question. I mean, why should I have one of my guns pointed at the nigga who rolled with my brother every single day out there in them streets? Both of you niggas petty hustling, hitting nothing ass licks. Then, all of a sudden, I give this nigga 4 birds, and he winds up dead, but his right-hand man don't know shit. So you right, I shouldn't have a gun pointed at you."

He grabbed the .45 off of his waist and slammed it on the table. "Bitch nigga, I should have two pointed at you, because if you don't tell me something to make me understand some shit, I'm emptying both clips. That's on my daughter." He frowned and picked up the bottle. "Speak, nigga!"

Jock never trusted T. He felt like him and his little brother never had shit in common. In T, he saw a nigga who was dead set on getting out of the hood. He saw ambition and a certain griminess. In his little brother, all he saw was a little nigga who would never understand the streets. He was a follower, and a nigga who constantly went in circles when he hustled. He saw a dependent. The only thing that stopped him from snatching up T and putting him down with his crew was the fact that he was so close to his brother.

Jock still loved him just like an older brother should have, and he wasn't accepting any nigga crossing his family and shedding their blood.

T didn't know what to say. He had so many things running through his head that he couldn't think straight. Sweat started to pour down his face. His heart was pounding in his chest, and he felt like he was going to faint.

"Bruh, I don't know what to tell you. If I knew anything, I would be down here singing like Usher right now. That was my nigga, and his death caught me off guard just like it did you. I'm down to do whatever to avenge it, but I didn't have nothing to do with it. That's on my kids."

"What happened to my bricks? Did you know he had them?" Jock asked with barely any emotion.

"Yo, what?" T asked perplexed.

Jock was tired of playing games. He had a feeling T knew more than he led on. He picked up the .40 and pulled the trigger. *Boom!* The bullet slammed into T's shoulder, knocking him out of the chair and on to his knees.

"Get yo' bitch ass back in that chair and answer my question!" T crawled on his knees with blood spurting out of his shoulder.

He felt trapped. The pain was so intense. He put his hand over the gunshot wound and felt the blood seep through his fingers. He slowly climbed to his feet and found his seat, looking at Jock with pure hatred.

"My dope, bitch nigga? Did you know about my dope?" He leaned down and tooted another line.

T nodded. "Yeah, but that shit ain't have nothing to do with me. Once bruh told me you gave him some work to serve, I already knew I wasn't fucking wit' it because I knew he'd fuck it off, then you'd want a nigga's head. Fuck that. I had a lick lined up that would get us about 50 G's, knocking off a nigga's safe who just went to the feds. His sons trying to get their weight up, but I was gon' rock they ass before they had a chance to." The pain shot through him, making him feel dizzy. There was a constant throbbing that had him ready to pass out.

56

"You talking 'bout Chauncey?" Jock mugged the shit out of him.

T swallowed, "Yeah, why is that a problem?" He whispered, fighting to stay awake. The blood loss was getting the best of him.

Jock mugged him. "That nigga's from Bankhead. That means most of his money is mine. If you was finna hit this nigga, then that means you was finna hit me, and I find it hard to believe if you'd hit me on the one hand, you wouldn't hit me on the other. Bitch nigga, you got snake in you, and in my garden, I exterminate snakes."

He stood up and aimed both barrels at him. "What you want me to tell yo' bitch, nigga?"

T breathed hard and opened his eyes to face Jock. He was panicking, but knew his life was over. He couldn't think of anything to say. He imagined his children and Star, and tears fell from his eyes. Star had been so good to him. He would miss her. He shook his head. "Just tell her I love her, and I'm sorry."

Jock nodded. "I got you."

Boom! Boom! Boom! Boom! The fire spit out of his gun, illuminating the basement.

It ended with T in a pool of his own blood, his eyes wide open. Jock sat back down at the table and finished his cocaine.

Ghost

Chapter 7

The door opened just as Jahrome was pulling down his mask. Claudia, a fine ass Rican chick with way too much makeup on, opened the door and smiled. "They up there right now. It's three of them, *papi*. Two of the Cobras, and one Asian dude. As soon as you get to the top of the stairs, you look to your left, and they'll be sitting at that table in front of the big plasma screen. Make sure you hit Hector's ass a few times. He killed my brother. I watched him do it." Her lips quivered before tears fell down her cheeks.

Rico nodded. "Cool. *Mamita*, wait for me in the car. It's parked in the abandoned garage four houses down. It's a black Caprice. Go." She nodded and ran off of the porch before running alongside the gangway leading to the back of the house.

"You ready to do this shit, papa?" Rico hunched down and looked up the stairs.

"Nigga, let's go." Jahrome said and adjusted his mask for the last time. He cocked his Glock and made his way up the stairs.

Once he got to the top, he peeked to his left, and saw all three men. They were sitting on a couch. Two of them were playing Fortnite, while the third sat back, counting a bundle of cash. The third one looked up from his money back to the television over and over as if he didn't want to miss what was taking place.

Jahrome nodded his head. He felt this was going to be a walk in the park.

Rico came and placed his back against the wall. He held a TEC-9 in his hand with a hundred-round magazine attached to it. His chest was already rising and falling as if he'd ran a full mile. "Aight, Jahrome, let's let these niggas know what it really is."

He nudged open the door, and frowned under his mask, before rushing inside with his arm outstretched. "Muthafuckas! Retaliation is a muthafucka!" He hollered in Spanish, and then his TEC was spitting round after round. Bullets popped into the air. Fire released from the barrel as his rounds began to chop down the three men with no remorse.

Jahrome took a deep breath, and ran inside of the apartment. He aimed and fired. His first round splitting the Asian's head down the middle. He took a step back, and allowed Rico to seek his revenge. After all, it appeared to be personal for him. Jahrome continued to survey the apartment to make sure they had everything under control.

Rico continued to spit until he chopped the men down to the ground. They lay in front of the television screen, gasping.

Rico stood over them and looked down. "You punk muthafuckas! How dare you kill innocent people? This shit ain't got nothing to do with little kids. Now look at you, *vato*."

He stepped over the two who were struggling for their lives, and finished them off. He held the smoking TEC in his hand. There were so many shells, it looked like he'd dropped a box of them by accident. He turned his back to his slain prey, and gave Jahrome a what up nod. "Say, are you good, homes?"

Jahrome nodded back at him. "I'm Gucci. I'm 'bout to snatch up these bank rolls though." He rushed over and started to stuff the money. He stuffed as much in his own bag as he could. Rico rushed beside him and started to do the same. They had taken all thirty bands. "Let's get the fuck out of here, mane. The Police gotta be on his way by now."

Rico shook his head. "Wait a minute. This is a safe house. I know for a fact they got a few birds in this mahfucka. I ain't finna leave until we come up on a few of them. It's only right we capitalize off of this hit. They would have done it to us, homes."

Jahrome waved him off. "You're out of your fuckin' mind. We need to get out of here, bruh. That was a lot of shooting. You already know them people are on the way. We'd be dumb as a muthafucka to stick around and see how long it'll take them to get here." Jahrome stepped into the hallway that led to the staircase. "Come on, bruh, let's bounce."

Rico wasn't having it. He had to make the hit more beneficial. That was how he was raised in the game. He felt any time there was bloodshed, there should be serious money gained from the carnage.

"Say, homes, you go on downstairs, and I'll meet you in the car. I'm gonna rush and tear this muthafucka up. I know for a fact there is at least ten birds in here." He turned his back to Jahrome and rushed into the kitchen. He grabbed a spare garbage bag from out of the garbage can and came back into the living room to see what Jahrome was doing.

Jahrome hung his head. He was irritated. He hated to have set out on a mission to accomplish one thing, and now, Rico was trying to change it and elongate the process. This made Jahrome want to snap and leave his ass behind.

"What's up, bro? I said you could go downstairs and wait in the car. It's all good. You've proven yourself. I'm going to fuck with you from here on out. Now go." Rico turned his back ready to go and search the back rooms.

Jahrome waved him off. He was over it. He took a step out of the apartment, and he was on the top stair when he saw a figure from the corner of his eye. He snapped his head to the left, and he saw a short Spanish girl with a .45 in her hand, easing out of the closet.

She came all the way out, aimed at Rico, and cocked her hammer. "You killed my brothers, you son of a bitch!" *Boom! Boom! Boom!*

"Riiiiiiiccccccoooooo!" Jahrome yelled, and ran back inside of the apartment. He aimed and hit her with slug after slug, flipping her around until she was facing him.

Rico struggled to crawl across the floor. He left a blood trail. His back felt as if it was on fire. He winced in pain, and laid still with his face in the crux of his arms. "That punk ass bitch got me. She got me, Jahrome." He closed his eyes, and dropped his TEC.

Jahrome knelt down and assessed the damage. He saw one hole in Rico's back. It was just before the center of his shoulder blades. "Fuck." He looked from left to right in a panic. "I told you we should've got the fuck out of here, Rico. Damn, nigga! Come on and get yo' ass up." He forced him to stand.

Rico felt the pain shooting all over his back. It hurt so bad that a tear left his eye and rolled down his cheek. "Get me the fuck out of here, Jahrome. Damn, I'm glad that you was wit' me. That bitch had me dead wrong. Don't forget my TEC." He pointed at the gun that lay in a puddle of blood.

Jahrome stopped and picked it up. He helped Rico make it to the stairs, and then helped him down. Every step they took, Rico winced and groaned from the pain shooting up and down his back.

Rico pulled his mask off. He felt like he couldn't breathe. He took in a gasp of air, and swallowed his spit. He now felt the pain shooting up and down the back of his legs. He was seconds away from going limp. When they got to the door, Rico buckled against him, and brought Jahrome to his knees.

"Get yo' ass up, nigga. Come on. We gotta get the fuck out of here."

Rico struggled to his feet. He picked up his head, and opened his eyes. Sweat slid down the side of his face.

He looked straight forward, and when his eyes came into focus, he saw two of the Cobra killers hopping over the fence. One had a revolver in his hand.

"Jahrome, look!" He pushed Jahrome away from him and fell backward. "Shoot them niggas!"

Jahrome looked up just as the hitta was getting ready to aim. He raised Rico's TEC and squeezed the trigger, running at the man *kamikaze* style.

"Ahhhhhhhhhhhh!" He yelled, holding the trigger. The hitta flew backward into the fence, while one bullet after the next entered his body. When the last one caught him between the eyes, he dropped his .357 and fell face first into the grass.

The other hitta jumped back over the fence and took off running. He'd been able to make out Rico. That was all he needed to see. He would spread word to the others, and Rico would pay.

Jahrome allowed Rico to wrap his arm around his neck, while he carried him back out to the car.

When they got there, Claudia jumped out of the back of the car in a panic. Her eyes were as big as saucers. "Oh my God! Oh my God! What happened to him?" She hollered.

Jahrome moved her out of the way with his free hand. "Fuck it look like? He's been shot. Jump in the passenger seat. I gotta get him to the hospital." Jahrome said, pushing Rico's legs inside of the car before he closed the door.

Claudia got into the passenger's seat, and covered her face with her hands. "We fucked up. We fucked up. I told Rico I didn't want to do this. Now look at him. They got him. They done shot you, *papi*, and it's all my fault."

Jahrome got behind the wheel of the car and started the ignition. "Shawty, shut yo' ass up. That nigga's good. You probably trippin' more than he is."

She covered her face again, and shook her head from side to side. "I can't. I just can't. Rico was my only hope at getting revenge for what they did to my brother, but I didn't mean to get him hurt in the process." She unbuckled her seat belt and climbed into the back seat so she could comfort him. She rubbed the side of his face. "I'm so sorry, *papi*. I'm so, so sorry. Please forgive me."

Jahrome drove down the alley and turned on to a residential street. He was trying to think of which hospital was the closest. "Say, Rico, which hospital you want me to take you to?"

Rico was losing blood at a fast pace. He was dizzy, and a bit disoriented. "You can't take me to no hospital, homes. Those fuckers there will call the *policia* for sure. I'm not trying to go down for those murders, homes. Just take me to one of my bitch's cribs. She's a doctor. She'll take this slug out of me for sure. She stays over on Pike Drive, the first red-bricked house on top of the hill." He closed his eyes again, and winced in pain. He was beginning to feel cold.

Jahrome nodded his head and obeyed. Claudia continued to hold Rico's head in her lap. "This is all my fault. I should have thought things through."

She locked eyes with Jahrome in the rearview mirror. "Why is he the only one shot? How did you manage to escape unscathed?" She snapped bitterly.

Jahrome ignored her. He jumped on the highway and stepped on the gas. Babygirl kept crossing his mind. He was praying she was okay. He also thought about Mami. He didn't know how he was going to tell her her brother had been shot, but he knew he had to figure things out quickly.

"Hey, muthafucka! You hear me talking to you up there? How is it that Rico has been shot, and your black ass has come from under all of this untouched? It just doesn't make any sense. Now I want some answers, or I swear to God something bad is going to happen to you. You better hope he makes it. I mean it."

Jahrome eyed her from his mirror. "Bitch, shut up. You starting to get on my muthafuckin' nerves. Shut yo' goofy ass up, and sit back. I ain't gon tell yo' ratchet ass again."

"Ratchet? I know you ain't just call me ratchet. Do you have any idea who you're talking to?" She asked, rolling her neck as Jahrome pulled off of the freeway and came to a red light.

"Bitch, hell naw, and I don't give a fuck who either. Sit yo' ass back, and let me get bruh's ass to this doctor in peace. I got too much shit on my mind to be worrying about you back there working on my fuckin' nerves. Shut yo' trap."

"Fuck you, nigga! You don't know me! I ain't gotta do shit but stay Puerto Rican and die." She rolled her eyes, closed them for a dramatic effect, and popped her neck.

Before she could open her eyes, she felt the cold barrel of his Glock slammed to her forehead. She yelped. "Yeah, bitch, you're most definitely right about the last part. Good night." He squeezed the trigger, and shot her in the head, getting blood all over Rico's chest.

Rico slowly opened his eyes. "I was wondering when you was finna waste this bitch. You already knew we couldn't let her just roam free no way." He pushed her limp body off of him. "Hurry up now, bruh. I'm losing too much blood."

Jahrome turned around, and stepped on the gas, driving past the lights. He was thankful for the peace and quiet.

"Rico, while you're getting patched up, I'ma take care of Claudia, and make sure the girls are straight. You just hold on. Everything is under control."

Rico smacked his lips. "I know, bruh. I know. A mahfucka appreciate you more than you'll ever know. I think Mami found herself a..." His eyes crossed before he fainted. Both him and Claudia wound up on the floor in a puddle of their own blood. Jahrome stepped on the gas and headed for Pike Drive.

Chapter 8

Babygirl looked back at her reflection in the mirror and took another deep breath. She had put on as much makeup as she could, yet the scar was still visible. She blinked back tears, and tried her best to wipe them away without smearing her work.

"This just gon' have to do." She said to herself, feeling defeated.

Jahrome stepped into the bathroom and kissed her on the cheek, catching her off guard. "Hey, what's the matter, sis? Why you looking so down?" He asked with concern.

She shook her head. "Hey, I didn't hear you come in. I gotta go get this money. It's gon' be my first day back at the club, and I'm just worried about how everybody finna react to the shit this nigga did to me. I don't think I can deal." She said, lowering her head, and swallowing before looking at her reflection.

Jahrome took a deep breath and wrapped her into his arms. "That's because I wanted to surprise you. And you really don't even gotta go back to that weak ass club. I already told you I got you. I'll go out there in them streets and make shit happen for us. You know how I get down." He hugged her tighter and kissed her cheek.

She felt so safe and secure in his arms. It seemed like he was the only one who understood her pain. He always tried to be her sacrifice ever since they were kids. She appreciated and loved her brother, her protector. "You shouldn't always have to make shit happen on your own. After all, I'm your big sister. I'm supposed to be looking out for you, not the other way around." She leaned back into him.

"You know you still just as beautiful, right? You know there ain't no woman as beautiful walking this Earth. Ain't nobody got nothing on you, Babygirl. I mean that. Them ma'fuckas in that club oughta be happy to have you dancing for them, because you don't have to be. I'd take care of you the rest of my life if I had to because I love you."

She closed her eyes and moved backward into his arms. She loved how secure she felt in his arms. She felt complete, and she couldn't understand why. Along with all of those feelings, she also felt guilty because it was him making her feel so whole.

"I love you, too, lil' bro, and I thank you for your kind words. You always know what to say to make me feel better. You always have." She said, the last part barely above a whisper.

He turned her around so that she faced him, rubbing his thumb up and down her cheek. "You know you ain't gotta go out there tonight, right? You know I'll figure shit out. I'll make sure that you are able to keep maintain the lifestyle that you're used to living. I'll keep you spoiled because you deserve that."

He was serious. He didn't want her out there trying to make it happen in a world based on looks. He didn't know how he would react if she came back home with a broken heart. In his eyes, the scar didn't take away from her beauty at all. But then again, he was crazy about her.

She was his everything. The world would see her differently. The world would judge her off of looks, and attack. He knew she wasn't strong enough for that.

Babygirl blinked back tears, and wrapped her arms around his neck, laying her cheek against his chest. "I know you would, and I know I don't have to go out here, but I want to because I gotta face this world one day. Why not make today that day?"

It had only been 2 weeks since the attack, and her scar looked fresh. Though the stitches had been taken out, they didn't help. The makeup only masked so much.

Jahrome nodded. "Well, if you gotta do what you gotta do, then handle yo' business. When you get back here, I'll be here for you with arms wide open." He kissed her on the forehead and held her for another five minutes in silence, until she was strong enough to finished getting dressed.

* * *

Before Star could make too much noise, Jock decided to hit her ass up, and find his dope. So he surprised her in the middle of the night with a slap to her face and yanking her hair before Gunz , his bodyguard, put her in a sleeper hold. Gunz also duct taped her kids' mouths and laid them on the floor of her bedroom. Jock threw another shoebox out of the closet, and took all of the clothes and threw them across the room. "I know this nigga left my shit here wit' you, Star. Now you finna tell me what's good, or I'm finna have the homie break your bones one at a time." He continued fucking her closet up that she had shared with T.

It was four o'clock in the morning, and Jock was on a rampage. Three days after he killed T, Star was going crazy looking for him.

"Jock, I swear to you, I don't know anything. I don't know what he had going on. I'm just his woman. Please don't hurt me or my children." She whimpered, scared for her babies' lives.

She knew Jock was a lunatic. The city of Atlanta knew it, too. The last thing she needed was for him to screw her family over. Now she was starting to wonder if he had something to do with T coming up missing.

Jock flipped over the bed in anger. "Bitch, that ain't what I wanted to hear. Now, you just getting on my nerves with these lies. That nigga is soft. He the type who listens to everything his bitch says. So that means that you were running the show. I ain't stupid." He frowned at her, breathing hard. "Gunz, break that bitch's wrist." he ordered.

Gunz picked Star up in the air and slammed her on her back, before straddling her. He took a piece of duct tape and placed it across her mouth, before grabbing her left arm.

Star screamed into the tape, fearing for her well-being. She felt him take a hold of her wrist and snapped it backwards.

"Arrrgh! Arrrgh!" The pain was so unbearable that she began to shake.

Jock sat on the bed and laughed. "That's why I keep this big ass nigga around. That shit hurts, don't it? Fuck, I bet it do." He put fire to his blunt and shook his head. "Now, he finna take that tape off of your mouth, and you gon' tell me where my shit at, and what happened to my brother, or I'm gon' have the homie break your forearm. Now that's the bone of bones. You have that ma'fucka break, and shit gets real. Trust me on that." He took a strong pull from the ganja, and inhaled.

Pull that tape back a lil' bit so I can hear this bitch." Gunz followed directions. He gripped Star by the back of the neck so hard that his nails dug into her skin, causing her to bleed. With pain shooting up from her wrist, Star was out of breath. It felt like she was about to die, and she was scared. "Jock, he never told me about any dope. Never, I swear he didn't. If he would have told me anything, I would have told you everything by now. My loyalty is to my kids, not to a man. Believe me on that."

Jock shook his head. He still wasn't believing that shit. He knew from experience that Star was a compulsive liar. They had went to school together, and her and Dymond were close.

One time, Star had gotten mad at him for flexing on her ass, and she told Dymond he tried to get at her, which he never did. He had secretly never forgiven her for that, but had let shit go because of Dymond. Now, he felt like getting a little revenge, and reminding her of her transgressions. He blew the thick smoke to the ceiling and dumped the ashes on the carpet. "Say, Star, do you remember when we was all back in high school, and I told everybody you was sewing yo' Tommy Hilfiger signs on in yo' mom's kitchen?"

Star swallowed, and tried her best to not think about the pain shooting from her wrist. "Yeah, I remember that, Jock. That wasn't cool. You had everybody shitting on me all year. I hated my sophomore year because of that." She could feel the tears rolling down her cheeks.

"Do you remember what you told Dymond to get back at me?" He asked, mugging her with hatred.

She closed her eyes tightly. She remembered exactly what she had told Dymond, and she was starting to figure out where he was about to take things.

She panicked. "Jock, that was so long ago. I already apologized to you and my girl. You know I would never get down like that again. I'm sorry. Please just let me--"

"Break her shit in half, my nigga, but put that tape over her mouth first." Jock ordered and looked on in anticipation. Gunz nodded, and knelt down, putting the tape across her mouth.

He grabbed her arm, and put his knee against it, pulling backward with all of his might with his eyes closed. Star's eyes were wide open. She screamed under the tape. She could hear her bones cracking. The pain shot up and down her arm, and caused the hairs on the back of her neck to stand up. The more he pulled, the worse the pain got until she heard a loud snapping sound, and her forearm folding in against his massive knee before the pain was too much to bear.

She screamed her heart out, with her eyes rolling into the back of her head. The top of her hand rested against her elbow. The bone showed through her skin like wood poking through a plastic bag.

Jock laughed on the bed and clapped his hands together. "That's that shit I'm talking about! Now that's how you get results. I want you to do the other one the same way. Do that shit. Damn, this a good ass movie!"

Star tried to fight against him. She didn't know how much more she could take. She was in so much pain that she wanted to die. She wanted to be anywhere but here. She hated her life.

She hated T for getting her into the bullshit with Jock. She hated Jock for holding a grudge against her after they had been out of high school for almost five years. It wasn't fair.

Gunz grabbed her right arm, and forced his knee against it in the same way he had done the first one, but this time he pulled with so much of his strength that he snapped her entire forearm in half, before yanking her up by a handful of hair.

Star was shaking uncontrollably while he held her in front of Jock. Her freshly painted toenails dug into the carpet of her bedroom. She shook uncontrollable as drool coming seeped from the corners of her mouth. Her body was going into shock. All the pain was too much to handle.

Jock stood up and smacked her with all of his might, shifting her focus. "Bitch, wake yo' ass up, and tell me something. This shit ain't a game. Now where the fuck my bricks at, and what happened to my brother?"

He walked across the room and picked up her oldest son, Temarco, who was 9 years old. He held the boy by his throat in front of Star, and slid his .44 Desert Eagle down his throat, causing him to choke.

He could feel the little boy shaking like crazy, and it only excited him. "Bitch, this is yo' last warning. From here on out, every time I ask you a question, and you don't give me the answer, somebody gon' die. Now where are my bricks? What happened to my brother? Answer my questions in that order."

Star could barely think straight. She was so tired. The pain was too much. Sweat dripped down her back, and pooled along the waistband of her yellow boy shorts. She didn't know what to say. Gunz snatched the tape off of her mouth.

"You steady getting at me. Why you ain't ask him? Or why you ain't ask Babygirl? That bitch nigga tell her more shit than mine do. We was all together the night before he got killed.

We was at her house. I was drunk, and passed out. I heard he fucked her up real bad. Maybe her brother took a good look at the nigga. He didn't like him, and they never got along. Maybe he kilt him, and took yo' dope or something. I don't know." She said, out of breath.

Jock turned his head to the side. "What's this nigga's name?" He asked, intrigued.

Her eyes rolled into the back of her head, and she wanted to faint. "His name's Jahrome. He was in the ninth grade when we were all seniors. A yellow nigga with hazel eyes. Babygirl is his sister. They stay over on Center Street, outside of Woodlawn. That nigga's a goon, just like you." After saying this, she fell and Gunz had to pick her back up.

"Oh, you think he a goon like me, huh?" He pushed her son's face as close to her as possible. *Boom! Boom!* He blew the back of his head out, before dropping him and kicking him in the stomach.

"Bitch! You been withholding this information! You could have told me this shit!" He started to smack her in the face with the pistol, but it was too late.

Star simply couldn't take any more. She kept seeing the back of her baby's head exploding. She was his mother, and she was supposed to save him. She was supposed to protect him, but she had failed, and now, her heart was failing her. Life had dealt her all that she could handle. She went into cardiac arrest, shaking and convulsing.

Gunz dropped her and put two fingers to her neck, before shaking his head at Jock. Jock shrugged his shoulders, then knelt down, putting the pistol to the other boy's head, and pulling the trigger twice. *Boom! Boom!*

He felt no emotion at all. He had no attachments to the children because of Star. He held a grudge over the years, and in his mind, her kids were constant reminders of how he felt about her. He was thankful for the information though. He needed find a way to utilize it. But first they had to handle this Star and her son's body.

* * *

Babygirl lowered herself into John's lap and grinded him while he held on to her waist. Aaliyah's "One in a Million" played in the background. He had become one of her regulars at the club.

All throughout the club, bitches were getting it in, doing their thing to try and bring home as much money at the end of the night as possible. She had been at work for two hours, and was only at 75 dollars, when usually, she'd be in the high hundreds on her way to a thousand, and that was even on a slow day.

Her confidence was wavering. She knew it had to do with the scar on her face. She was trying her best to shut it out of her mind, but the other females in club kept on bringing light to it. The fact she was still under a hundred dollars was making it even more difficult to focus on anything else.

She felt John's hands slide up on his way to her breasts, but she stopped him. "Whoa, daddy. We got a no- touch policy at this club, so you can't be doing all of that." She leaned all the way forward and continued to grind in his lap.

He looked down and saw all of that ass and couldn't help rubbing it. He figured since she was facially fucked up, she'd appreciate him taking sympathy on her asking for a private dance. He felt that he should have been able to do anything that he wanted. She should have been grateful.

"Shawty, the reason I asked for this private dance is so my hands could do a little talking, you know what I mean?" He said, revealing a mouthful of gold.

Babygirl scrunched her face and looked back at him. "Like I said, ain't none of that shit allowed. So you gon' have to follow the rules, or we gon' have a problem."

John stood up and pushed her off of him. "Then I'm straight. Bitch, I can get a regular dance from one of these bad bitches in here. You think I'm finna pay you 50 dollas for you to shake yo' ass in my lap, and ain't shit popping? Bitch, please. Watch out." He slid from the couch, and moved her out of the way, damn near knocking her over.

Babygirl sat on the couch for a long time, looking around the club before Trinity came over and told her that she was up next on the main stage. She nodded and stood up, trying to build up her confidence.

She knew she had about ten minutes before she stepped on because Keila's set was just starting, so she rushed to her dressing room and pulled out her cellphone, calling her brother.

As soon as he picked up, her heart started to beat faster. "Hey, Rome, I just needed to hear your voice because I'm about to go out on the main stage for a set, and I'm feeling scared. I need your words of encouragement to get me through." She looked around the dressing room at a few of the girls who were naked and squeezing into their attire. Their bodies were flawless, along with their faces. She felt so defeated and lost.

"Babygirl, can you hear me?"

She nodded as if he could see her. "Yeah, I hear you."

"Babygirl, you are the baddest chick in that building. Ain't nobody got shit on you. You always been the coldest woman walking this earth, and ain't shit changed. Now, you already know I couldn't leave you out on a limb like that, so I'ma be sitting a few tables back in honor of you. I'm already here. You know I got you, boo."

She lowered her head, and blinked back tears. "I love you so much, Jahrome.Thank you."

"Don't thank me. Just come out here and do your thing. You got this. You are just beautiful as them other hoes."

Chapter 9

Ginuwine's "Pony" came on, and Babygirl was introduced to the stage. She took one last deep breath and pulled the purple curtain back. She stepped through it with a red and black Prada robe.

She stepped into the spotlight and wiggled her hips, before rolling her back seductively. Her tongue ran across her cherry-painted lips. She rolled her body like a snake, taking her hand and trailing it down her stomach, pulling the robe up a little bit to expose the see-through red panties underneath. Before coming out, she had purposely made sure that they were stuffed into her pussy lips.

As the song continued, she got a little bolder, sliding the robe off of her shoulders, dropping it to the floor. She walked sexily across the stage, taking her hands and cupping her titties through her matching see-through Prada bra, before opening it in the front.

Mami crept up behind Jahrome, putting a hand over his eyes. "You can't see all of that, *papi*. She's starting to get naked. Ooohwee!"

Jahrome smiled and moved her hand out of the way. "Man, I done seen my sister naked a million times. Get yo' mind out of the gutter."

Babygirl dropped down and hit the splits before coming up on all fours and turning her ass toward the crowd. She leaned forward and pulled her panties to the side, exposing her pussy. She tried to block out knowing Jahrome was in the audience, but every time she succeeded, it caused her confidence to slip.

The more she imagined she was dancing only for him, the stronger she felt. She pulled her panties off, and laid face-down on the stage, opening her pussy lips wide, revealing her pink insides.

Jahrome was trying his best to not feel aroused. Every time things would get too intense for him, he would close his eyes, but that didn't help because the last image he saw would only repeat. It was burned into his mind's eye.

Mami sat beside him on the couch and began stroking his thigh. Then she took her hand and slid it into his pants, before stroking his dick.

"Damn, this shit turning me on. I see your shit getting hard, too. It better be from what I'm doing, and not what she's up there doing. But then again, she got me wet as hell."

She squeezed her thighs together, and came forward on the couch, pulling Jahrome's dick out of his pants. She sank to the floor, taking him into her mouth.

Now shit was getting hectic for him. Mami was sucking him like her life depended on it, and Babygirl had her pussy lips spread so far apart he could see her hole. She made her ass clap, and started to twerk, with her titties jiggling like crazy.

Mami was sucking him hard and fast, licking up and down his shaft. She stroked it and squeezed it hard. It was huge in her little hand. It was throbbing, but she couldn't get enough of it in her little mouth, but she sure tried.

On stage, Babygirl's titties swung under her. Both nipples were rock hard from the cool air in the club. She reached behind and spread her ass, revealing both holes, then leaned all the way over.

They made eye contact, and he came all down Mami's throat. Glob after glob, and she sucked and swallowed with little effort. She stroked him in her tight fist, milking his dick. The forbidden aspect of it all drove her crazy.

* * *

Dymond paced back and forth in tears. It had been three days since she'd found out Star was murdered. She was her best friend, and she couldn't believe she was gone. They had discovered T's body a day before, and now, the hood was on edge. She had so many people hitting her up on Facebook from the old Bankhead neighborhood, inquiring about her friends, and she didn't know what to tell them. Not only did Star get killed, but both of her children had been bodied as well.

Jock came into the living room, holding their daughter, Aerial. She had her legs wrapped around him with her face in his shoulder and neck. She was a daddy's girl, and there was no doubt about that.

Dymond looked down at the red bottomed Guccis the little girl had on her feet. Everything Jock wanted her to have was top of the line. He always said that his daughter should have the best of everything.

"Is she asleep?" She asked.

He nodded, "Yeah, my baby's asleep. You know she can't resist that Midas touch." He smiled and kissed his little one on the cheek.

"Why you ask me that?" He said, laying her down on the couch. He decided to take a few days off from the streets while shit cooled down. He just wanted to lay back and chill, and spend some time with his daughter. He loved her with all of his heart.

"Because I want to talk to you about some things, and I want your honesty. I don't think she needs to be hearing all of that, so that's why I asked you." She rolled her eyes in irritation.

She felt like she was always competing with her daughter, and she hated it. She knew that he was crazy about his daughter, but she often felt ignored by him most times.

Jock sat down on the side of his daughter and rubbed her back while she slept. "Just holla at me, and I'll decide what she should and shouldn't hear. That's my baby right there. I ain't gon' keep telling you that."

Dymond swallowed. She didn't feel like making him mad. She knew once he lost his temper, it was horrible. Her only move was to change the subject.

"Okay, well, you know plenty of people been hitting me up asking about Star and them? Everybody been saying you run Bankhead, and nothing happens in Bankhead without you knowing about it. So you must know who bodied their whole family." She looked him over closely. "Do you?"

Jock picked Aerial up, and held her by the back of the head, gently bouncing her up and down.

"Bitch, go upstairs and get my belt, and wait for me in the room, because I done told you about gettin' in my bizness." Jock wasn't with the 21 questions and he definitely was going to teach diamond a lesson.

Dymond started to panic. The last thing she needed was an ass whooping from Jock, because sometimes he went so crazy that he wouldn't just land on her ass, but all across her back.

"Baby, I'm sorry. I was just curious." She ran to him and dropped to her knees at his feet, before wrapping her arms around his legs. "Baby, it's okay. I don't want to know anything. I know you're the man, and it's not my business. Let me just go in here and cook. Please."

Jock continued to bounce Aerial up and down. "Dymond, get yo' ass up and do what I said."

"Please, baby. I'm begging you." She whimpered. She didn't feel like going through all of that pain. She hated herself for always pushing the envelope with him. Nine times out of ten, if he wanted her to know something, he would tell her, but he didn't tell her much. That was just how he got down.

She felt him grabbing a handful of her hair. "Get the fuck up and do like I say!" He growled and pulled her to her feet by the hair.

"Daddeee, I'm scared!" Aerial said, waking up and looking down at her crying mother. "Is Mommy in trouble again?" She asked with her bottom lip quivering. She was used to her parents fighting, and it usually ended with her mother getting a whooping. She didn't like hearing her scream and cry. It made her sad.

"Don't worry about it, princess. This is Mommy and Daddy business. I'm going to lay you down in your room so you can get some sleep, or if you want, you can play on your tablet with your headphones on. But Mommy gotta get disciplined. That's just how it's going to go." He mugged the shit out of Dymond and told her with his eyes that he was finna wear that ass out.

He carried Aerial to her bedroom. He tried to let her down, but she kept her arms wrapped around his neck. He could hear the sounds of Jhené Aiko in the background on her sound system.

"Let my neck go, baby, so I can go and handle this business. You already know how your father gets down. Mommy hasn't been using her listening ears." He tried to pry her hands apart.

Aerial held his hands little tighter. "I don't want you to whoop her, Daddy. I don't like when Mommy cries. It makes me sad, and I want to help her because I be mad at you, even though I love you the most." She kissed his cheek. "Can't you just make her do a chore or something, so she don't have to get a whooping? I mean, for me, at least?" She looked into his eyes sadly.

Jock's heart fluttered. His baby girl was his everything, and she had such an effect on him. She was his sole purpose for getting up and going out into those streets and making it happen. She was so beautiful and innocent. He couldn't help but to melt in the presence of her.

She kissed his cheek again and rubbed his face with her small hand. "Daddy, are you mad at me?"

He shook his head. "No, baby, I'm not mad at you, but you have to understand that when Mommy messes up, she has to get a whoopin, or else she's going to keep on doing things that hurt this family. This is grown folks' business, and I really shouldn't be explaining it to you, but I love you, and I don't want you thinking that Daddy is whooping her for no reason."

He kissed her on the forehead. "So put your headphones on for a little while, and I'll go handle this." He hugged her tightly before leaving her room with a scowl on his face.

As soon as he got to his bedroom, he saw Dymond sitting on the edge of the bed with his leather belt on the side of her. She was curled up with her head on her chest, tears already rolling down her cheeks. He felt a little down that he was going to have to whoop her, ultimately disappointing his daughter, but he already knew the game that he was in.

Everyday, his life was on the line. People tried to find ways to get to him. They would not hesitate to squeeze his baby mother for answers, and anything she said would be used against them. As much as he valued his own life, nobody's life meant more to him than his daughter's.

Dymond handed him the belt as she watched him close the door. "Are you whooping me with my clothes on or off?" She asked, barely above a whisper. She was ready to get it all over with. She had mentally prepared herself for the pain.

Jock took a deep breath. He grabbed a handful of her hair, and flipped her on to her stomach. He pulled her skirt upward, exposing her pink G string. "I told you to mind yo' muthafuckin' bidness!" *Whap! Whap! Whap! Whap!*

He swung the belt through the air, before connecting with her naked skin again.

"Awww, Daddyy! I'm sorry! I'm sorry, Daddy!" She yelled and tried to get away from him.

She dove across the bed, and he grabbed her by the leg and pulled her back to him. *Whap! Whap!* The belt caused her ass cheeks to jiggle every time it crashed into them. It hurt like hell, but she had felt him do a worse job.

She wondered why he was taking it kinda easy on her. Jock brought the belt down again and started to feel uneasy. He was upset at the fact his daughter was probably listening to the way he was hurting her mother, causing him to feel bad on her behalf. It had nothing to do with Dymond because he wanted to tear her ass up, but he didn't want to hurt his princess. He wished she was at school, but they were on summer break.

He looked down and saw how Dymond's ass jiggled. No matter how angry he was, her body was his kryptonite. He reached and cupped her cheeks, kneading it like dough, loving the feel of it.

Dymond felt his caresses and bit into her bottom lip. As she laid on her stomach, she opened her legs wide to give him a peek of her treasures. She hoped that it would entice him to stop beating her.

Jock hopped on the bed, and grabbed a handful of her ass again, pulling the cheeks apart, before taking his fingers and playing with her asshole. "I know what I gotta do to you, because this belt don't work for that ass. Besides, I don't want my daughter hearing me doing that shit anyway."

He leaned down and bit her ass cheek, then opened her globes wider, and spit directly on her brown eye, smearing the spit into her hole, and fingering her back door swiftly.

"I'm finna fuck this ass until it's raw. That's what I'm finna do. I know you hate this big ass dick going in that booty." He smiled and saw the way her G string failed to cover her bald pussy lips. They were slightly open enough for him to view her pinkness.

Dymond's eyes got as wide as saucers. She started to think about him fucking her ass, and she wanted to scramble because every time he did, he was savage. She felt him fingering her ass hard, and she couldn't help but moan. It felt like at least three fingers. To prepare, she rubbed her clitoris, pinching it to send chills through her body. She closed her eyes, and sucked on her bottom lip.

Jock pulled her up by her hips, and pushed her face into the bed. After he stripped out of his shorts and boxers, he took his hard dick and trailed it up and down her slit, getting the head full of her juices before easing it into her backdoor.

"Hold that ass open for me." He growled. Dymond pulled herself wide open and felt him entering into her. It felt a little painful, until she started rubbing her clit furiously, and then she invited the intrusion. She yearned for it. "Uhhh, yeah, daddy. Fuck me, then." She moaned with her eyes closed.

Jock curled his upper lip. "Bitch, this ain't finna be that."

He slammed his dick all the way home and started to pound that ass out at full speed while she yelped and cried under him. Her asshole was gripping his dick like a fist. He saw how she played with her clit, and it encouraged him to go into beast mode. He sped up the pace.

Dymond couldn't take it. Her big ass wobbled and shook on her small waist. Her face rubbed back and forth across the sheet. Her mouth wide open, she felt him digging her out.

84

It was painful, yet at the same time, it felt so good that she couldn't help but to come hard.

Jock started to jerk. He could feel himself about to explode in that big booty. The way it shook and the way it felt when it bounced back into him, plus the heat and grip was all too much. He felt it all in his toes, and then, it was coming. He pushed her away from him. She landed on her stomach.

He pulled his dick out, and came all over the small of her back and thighs. Dymond felt the drops raining down on her body, and it turned her on even more. She jerked on the bed as another orgasm shot through her. Jock grabbed her by the throat and explained to her what it meant to stay in her lane.

Ghost

Chapter 10

Mami kissed Jahrome on the chest, and rubbed his rippling abs, before going to make breakfast. They spent the whole night fucking like rabbits, after leaving the club the night Babbygirl performed so well on stage. She was sore. She kissed his lips, and immediately smelled her scent on them. That made her smile.

She shook her head because she was becoming obsessed. She couldn't help herself. He was so amazing.

Just as she opened the bedroom door, Babygirl was in the doorway with her knuckles balled up as if she was about to knock. "Oh, girl, my bad. I was just about to see if y'all was up." She said, smiling.

"*Buenos días, mamita.* He's in there still sleeping, but you can go and wake him up since I'm about to have breakfast ready in a minute anyway. So you're good."

She kissed her on the cheek, and swished her hips all the way into the kitchen, rocking a pair of bikini-cut Burberry panties, and a half of a shirt that showcased the bottom of her breasts.

Babygirl had to admit Mami was a bad bitch in every sense of the word. She hoped the woman wouldn't fully steal her brother from her. As crazy as it sounded, she was overly jealous of her. She didn't like sharing her brother.

She went into the bedroom and closed the door behind her. She thought about locking it but decided that it would be too much.

She climbed on the bed and looked down on her brother as he slept peacefully. His handsome face looked as if it was in a state of euphoria. She laid beside him, and ran her hand across his rock hard abs, all the way up to his chest, before leaning down and kissing it. Then she laid her head on it and continued to rub his stomach. She loved him so much.

She never wanted to lose him. She was starting to feel some type of way about sharing him with Mami. Before she had come into the picture, Jahrome had spent most of his time with her.

Jahrome opened his eyes and looked down. He saw black, curly hair under him, and smelled the scent of Prada. It appealed to his senses.

He opened his eyes, "Damn, how long was I asleep?" He stretched a little before wrapping his right arm around her.

Babygirl shrugged her shoulders. "I don't know, but too long, if you ask me. I missed you. I've been going through it this morning, and I need for you to uplift me." She kissed his chest, and scooted closer to him, rubbing his abs, and nuzzling her face into his neck, drinking in his manly scent.

Jahrome hugged her possessively. "Well, I love you, and I hope you know you're the most beautiful girl in all the world. I'd die for you, and I'd kill a nigga over you quick. You're my everything, and there is nothing in this world I wouldn't do for you." He kissed her forehead.

"I love you, too. I think I love you too much. So much I can't control myself around you. I don't want to share you with anybody. I don't care who you are to me."

Babygirl closed her eyes and accepted his kiss. Something in her was going crazy. Every time he told her what he would do for her, or about her and how beautiful she was, it sent sparks through her body. Sparks she couldn't understand.

Before she knew it, she straddled him, with her gown raising around her hips. She leaned down and kissed his lips, and then she bit into his neck, and ground her pelvis into him hard. She moaned, and sucked his neck, reaching back and pulling her gown all the way up, with no panties on.

"Jahrome was caught off guard. He felt her hot body on top of him, and her kisses all over him. Mix that with morning wood, and he felt trapped.

He could feel her grinding into him, and as much as he wanted to push her off of him, he didn't. He didn't think she could stand the rejection. He didn't think it should have been him who knocked her down a few pegs, so instead, he reached and gripped her ass, and pulled her further into him, while she sucked all over his lips, moaning into his mouth.

"Umm, baby. I'm so sorry. I know I'm bogus, but I can't help it. I don't want to share you. I need you all to myself, and I want you so bad. I need you." She moaned, pulling her gown up and rubbing her hot pussy all over his stomach.

Jahrome felt the animal starting to come out of him. He felt himself losing the battle of good and evil. She needed him, and he wanted to be needed by her. Nobody meant more to him than his sister. She was his life. He gripped that booty so hard that he left marks all across it.

Babygirl fell on her side and slipped her hand between them, taking a hold of his huge penis, squeezing it, before stroking it up and down. She was getting ready to kiss the head when Mami called them from the kitchen.

"*Papi! Mamita!* It's time to eat, and I done put it down, so y'all betta get out here and fuck this shit up!" She yelled, her voice getting closer.

Jahrome's piece rested against Babygirl's cheek. She was caught between allowing them to get caught so Mami would disappear forever and doing what was right.

By the time Mami opened the door, Babygirl was standing on the side of the bed, and Jahrome was sitting up. She ran over to him and hopped on the bed beside him, wrapping her arms around his neck. "Good morning, *papi*. I hope you had a good night's sleep. I can fill that tummy up. I love you."

Babygirl stepped out of the room and into the hallway. She went into the guest room, falling to the floor with her arms wrapped around her knees, crying. She wanted Jahrome all to herself.

* * *

"How is your back feeling, *papi?*" Kelly, Rico's cousin asked, opening the passenger door to Rico's gold Tahoe truck. They were just coming from Junior's Burritos.

It was 80 degrees, sunny, and just a tad humid. Rico popped the lock, and opened his driver's side door, before unlocking the back doors so his little cousins could get in. He had been promising for weeks to take all of them out to the movies and for a bite to eat. He had been missing in action ever since the incident with his back. Though he sustained minor injuires, he had to be careful. Though his back was killing him, he wanted to keep his word.

His cousins, Ryan and Jacob, jumped into the back of the truck and immediately put on their headphones, playing games on their phones, and not paying attention to anyone.

Rico nodded. "It's cool. It still hurts at times like a son of a bitch, but I'm alive. That's all that matters."

Kelly got all the way into the truck and put her head against the headrest. "You're living a dangerous life, *papi*. Sooner or later, you're going to have to slow down, or you're going to leave the mother of your child to raise your boys all by herself. That ain't cool." She put on her seatbelt.

She loved her cousin with all of her heart. Every time she needed him, he was always there for her. After her husband, Roberto, was murdered by the Clayton Cobras, Rico stepped in and made sure she never worried about a bill again. All of the clothes on her and her children's backs were because of him, too.

"I love you. I hope you know that, Rico. You're good to me. You always have been." She reached over and brushed his cheek with the back of her hand.

Rico took her hand and kissed the back of it. "We're family. It's my duty to make sure you're good. I would be less than a man if I didn't do what I'm supposed to."

* * *

Arturo had been following Rico the whole day, waiting for the right time to end his life. The Cobras had put him in charge of personally knocking the man's head off. If he was able to do it, he would move up in the ranks.

Arturo looked over his shoulder at the van full of savages behind him. He smiled briefly before his smile turned into a sneer. "Looks like we caught that fool Rico slipping." He took the .40 from under his seat and cocked it.

"What you fellas think? I say we take care of this pretty boy right here and right now." Behind him, the men began cocking their firearms, preparing for war.

***

Rico counted out fifty singles after he pulled into the gas station. "Hey, anybody want anything to drink while I'm in here?"

Kelly smiled, and rested her hand on his shoulder. "Naw, *primo*, we're fine. Just go in and hurry up so we can make the movie on time. The last time we were late, the boys--"

There was a small tinkling sound, and then Kelly's face exploded. Her head jerked backward violently, before it wound up resting on the dashboard, leaking. Her sons began hollering at the top of their lungs, and then, the truck was under full attack.

Arturo rocked his gun, bussing at Rico's truck again and again, as his men stood behind him, spraying their fully-loaded, automatic assault rifles. "Ricoooo! You bitch ass nigga! *Bock. Bock. Bock. Bock.*

The windshield shattered. Rico felt four slugs slam into his chest, knocking him backward against the seat, and then all of the windows in the truck were breaking. Rico got low and started the truck, switched gears, and stepped on the gas.

Arturo and his men kept firing, chopping the truck with bullet after bullet. They busted Rico's brake lights and his back window. Somehow, Rico made it out of the gas station lot, and down the alley that was alongside the station. He floored the truck, thankful he'd been smart enough to wear his bulletproof vest that morning.

He felt sick to his stomach as he glanced over at Kelly. His little cousins were no longer hollering in the backseat, and he already knew what that meant. When he was far away from the attack scene, he pulled over the truck and got out.

He opened the backdoor to his whip, and sank to his knees as he saw the bullet-riddled bodies of Ryan and Jacob.

"Noooooo, God, no!" He sank his head. "They were just kids!"

Chapter 11

Jock slammed his hand down on the table, and looked around the room at the thirty niggas who stood looking up to him as if he were a god. In his hands were twin .40 Calibers. Across his chest was an all-white, Kevlar armored vest. He had his Atlanta Braves cap on backwards, with a red diamond stud in each ear. Around his neck, he wore his daughter's face in gold, encrusted with pink diamonds.

"Now there's plenty ma'fuckas asking me what took place with my little brother, and that nigga, T. The reason I called this meeting is because I want some answers. I wanna know what happened to my people. And not only that, I wanna know what y'all niggas ready to do about it."

He dipped the mini spoon into the cocaine in front of him and tooted it up hard. He looked around the room.

A goon named D-boy shrugged his shoulders. "Ma'fuckas talking like it could have been them niggas over there on 49th. They say yo' lil' brother ran into one of their spots a few months back, and niggas was hollerin' they was gon' get up wit' him sooner or later. Sounds to me it was sooner."

Jock leaned his head down and snorted a line of raw before pinching his nostrils. Jock mugged D-boy for a long time. "Nigga, how many times you done saw me since this shit happened to my brother?" He walked around the table toward him.

He shrugged his shoulders again. "I don't know, maybe three of four. Why is that important?" He scrunched his face, and felt himself getting a little irritated. It was super hot in that basement, and there were so many bodies down there, it only made it worse. D-boy was a fat nigga, so him and heat didn't get along at all. Jock was getting on his nerves.

Jock stopped in front of him, and looked at him like he had lost his mind. "What the fuck you just say?" He had to hear it again, just to make sure the 17-year-old had said what he said.

D-boy didn't want to let him punk him out in front of all of the savages of Bankhead, so even though he was scared for his life, he felt it in his best interest to put up a front. "I said, why do that--"

Jock took the handle of his pistol and slammed it into D-boy's head so hard it put a dent in the center of it. He swung the handle again, and put another hole right to the left of it, the same size.

D-boy jerked his head back as the pain rushed him at full speed. The blood spurt out of his wounds and dripped into his eyes, freaking him out. Then, Jock grabbed him by his long dreads and smacked him with the pistol so hard it cracked his jaw. Before he could digest that blow, more came in a flurry.

"Fuck you think you talking to, nigga! You think this shit a game? You think a ma'fucka killing my brother shouldn't be taken seriously? Huh?"

He beat him over and over again. The handle slammed into his cranium, and blood spurt across the concrete. Devin, D-boy's older brother, stood up. He was the reason D-boy was plugged into the Bankhead chapter of the ATL. Watching Jock beat his brother was making it hard for him to just stand by. "Yo, Jock, chill, nigga! You killing my lil' brother!"

Jock wrapped his hand around D-boy's throat and squeezed with one hand. He paused for a second, with D-boy's blood running down his face. He paid it no mind.

"Nigga, you betta sit yo' ass down, and stay out my bidness." He mugged him for a few seconds, felt D-boy stirring under him, and continued his assault. He cracked his head open.

94

D-boy was in so much pain. He prayed his big brother would step in soon. He was getting dizzy. Jock slammed the barrel of the gun into his mouth and cocked it.

"This nigga wanna hold information from me about my brother. Everybody thinks this shit a game. I'm a muthafucking chief, and you niggas ain't on shit. Y'all supposed to be tearing this city up on behalf of the god." He spit into D-boy's face.

Devin couldn't take anymore. He came at Jock full speed, and a few dudes grabbed him, held him back, ready to fuck him up.

Jock glared at Devin. "Naw, y'all let that bitch nigga go." He put both pistols on his waist.

"You think it's sweet, nigga? You think I need all these niggas to do my dirty work? Well I'll tell you what, if you whoop me, then I'll let your brother live. But if I beat yo' ass like I'm fin' to, then I'm killing you, and that bitch ass nigga." He paused and pointed at another fat nigga. "And him, too, since he's your cousin, and him, since that's his brother. We gone start wiping out whole bloodlines in this mafucka since ain't nobody respecting mine, so let's go, fat nigga. I ain't gotta use these pistols."

Devin looked around the room as everybody closed him into a circle in the big basement. He wished he never got involved with Jock. The niggas on the east side told him he could have jumped down with them, but he had gone against his better judgment and fucked with Bankhead. Now, his little brother was on the ground fighting for his life, and he was forced to go toe-to-toe with the chief of the whole hood, and he knew it would not end well.

"Yo, I don't want no problems wit' you, Jock. Just let me grab up my brother, and no hard feelings. Y'all will never hear from us again."

Jock snickered and curled his upper lip. "Really?" He stepped forward and busted him so hard in his mouth that Devin flew backward into the crowd of men, and they pushed him back in front of Jock. Jock caught him two times in the ribs, once in the stomach, then backhanded him, splitting the corner of his mouth. He could taste the blood. "Looks like you finna die, nigga. You and all these niggas related to you in the room." He adjusted the guns in his band again, and tucked in his chain.

Devin had tears in his eyes. He shook his head. "Man, Jock, just let us go, man! I'll fuck this city up for you. Just let me and my people survive this one. Please, man. I'm begging you."

Jock smacked him like a bitch. "You soft, nigga! You a pillow ass nigga. Scared to fight on behalf of your own people! How the fuck I'm supposed to trust you to fight and kill for me?" He swung and busted his nose.

"Arrrgh!" Devin ran at him, picked him up so high in the air that his head hit one of the pipes that ran along the ceiling. His head snapped backward. Devin slammed him down, and straddled him, raising his fist in the air. *Boom! Boom! Boom!*

Jock pushed him off of him and jumped up with blood running down his forehead. He aimed his guns at his face. *Boom! Boom! Boom!* Fire spit from the guns, causing the basement to light up again and again.

Devin jerked on the pavement as the bullets filled his body. It felt like hot fire piercing him. He got dizzy and struggled to breathe.

Jock saw the man's chest still rising and falling. He stepped over him and pulled the trigger again, ending his life, then emptying one of his clips into his brother.

"Now, let's talk about my brother! And every time niggas don't take me serious about what the fuck I got going on, I'm killing whole families from here on out."

* * *

Jahrome had stepped into a steamy shower when Mami ran into the bathroom and dropped to her knees.

"*Papi*, my brother's been shot again! Somebody shot him and killed my cousins! I don't know what to do, *papi*. I can't take it if he dies!" She whimpered, feeling like she was about to become hysterical.

Jahrome jumped out of the shower, and squatted down, pulling her into his arms. His wet body soaked her dry clothes. He felt her pain and wanted to heal her in any way that he could. "Baby, just tell me what you want me to do. Tell me and it's done because I got you." He moved her long, curly hair out of her face.

Mami stood up, and he followed. Wrapping her arms around the top of his neck, she laid her head on his chest. "Everybody trying to kill him, *papi*. Everybody wants my brother dead, and I don't know why because he's a good man. He does all he can for our family. If he gets killed, I'll just…" She sunk to the floor, sobbing.

Boom! Boom! Boom! Boom! The bathroom windows shattered.

Dymond screamed, "Jahrome! Help me! Where are you?" She'd been chilling in the living room when the shoots got her off guard.

Jahrome had thrown his body on top of Mami. *Boom! Boom! Boom! Doooom!* It sounded like something had exploded in the front room, and that caused him great concern. Was it Jock and his army, or was it somebody trying to kill off Rico's people?

He picked Mami up and placed her in the tub. "Stay down, baby. Don't move until I come back here and get you. Do you understand me?"

She nodded with tears in her eyes. "*Papi*, please don't leave me in this house. I'm so scared."

Ba-boom! Ba-boom! Ba-boom! Ba-boom! Ba-boom! The house rocked. Large chunks of wood flew from the walls.

The only thing on Jahrome's mind was saving his sister. He got on his stomach and crawled into the hallway as the shots continued to ring out.

"Babygirl, where are you?" He hollered, making his way to Mami's bedroom. Babygirl was under the bed, scared for her life. She had never heard so much gunfire.

She just knew it had to be Jock coming at them for Reggie's murder.

She heard about what happened to Star and her children, and T, and it freaked her out. She didn't want them to end up like them. "I'm in Mami's room, Jahrome. Hurry!" She screamed as the shots rang louder.

Jahrome made it to the room, and looked under the bed. His sister was curled into a ball, crying like a little baby. It broke his heart. He stuck his head underneath and kissed her on the forehead, as they heard the tires screeching away.

Fifteen minutes later, they were on the highway with Mami behind the wheel while he held his traumatized sister in the back seat.

"It's gon' be okay, Babygirl. We just gotta get the fuck out of here for a little while. Shit real hot, and Rico and I gotta handle some business."

They had to handle some business, or all of them would be in grave danger.

"Yeah, don't trip, Babygirl. We're going to go chill with my grandmother. She's cool people, and there's no drama over there. We'll be there for a few days until we can find out what we're going to do." Mami said.

Babygirl heard what she was saying, and what irritated her was the "we," all three of them. She hated that Mami kept on linking herself in with her and Jahrome. All Babygirl cared about was being in his arms. She hoped that the ride took an eternity, so he could hold her for as long as possible.

Jahrome kissed her cheek, and ran his thumb across it. "I love you, sis. I'll never let anything happen to you again. You hear me?" He rubbed his face against hers, and held her more firmly.

He was ready to kill some shit. He was tired of being on the receiving end.

Mami looked into her rearview mirror as she switched lanes. She couldn't help feeling a little jealous at Jahrome holding Babygirl instead of her. She was shaken up too, and needed a bunch of consoling. She didn't like that she was hogging her man.

She understood Babygirl had been through a lot over the last month, but she felt she needed him more, and that it was his job to be there for her. Every girl needed a protector, and she had one. She just wished that Babygirl found her own.

"Jahrome, don't give all of your love away. You know I need you too, *papi*." She said.

Jahrome felt Babygirl's hand go up his shirt, and it made him hug her tighter. She rubbed his stomach, and he did his best to turn his back to Mami to block what Babygirl was doing. "Aw, you know I'll never do that, baby. I got you as soon as we get there. I know you need me, and I need you too. So never forget that."

Mami smiled and focused on the road. She couldn't wait to make it to Atlanta. She had plans on being all under her man. She just needed to feel his big arms wrapped around her.

Babygirl ran her fingers along the waist of his pants, before sliding one of them in and against his lower abdomen. She could feel his heat, and it turned her on.

She tried to force her whole hand down his pants. She just wanted Mami to catch them so she could go about her business.

Jahrome grabbed her wrist and squeezed it, whispering in her ear. "Sis, chill. You know I got you. You just hurting right now, and you're acting out. We gon' talk."

Babygirl heard the words, and blinked back tears. She didn't know why she was behaving this way, but she felt like she couldn't help it. After the incident with Reggie, she didn't want to lose the only man in the world who really cared about her and found her beautiful. She felt like she needed him way more than Mami did.

She squeezed his thigh and whispered, "Jahrome, will you ever leave me? Will you ever leave my side, and leave me all alone in this cold, cold world? Be honest." She felt so vulnerable.

Jahrome held her tightly. "Never." he whispered. "You're my everything. We've always been all that we've had. You have always been there for me, and I love you." He kissed her cheek.

Babygirl felt shivers run through her body. Every kiss made her feel weaker and stronger at the same time. The more she thought she should let go, the more she held on. Jahrome was like her heartbeat. She needed him just as much.

Mami looked into her rearview mirror again. "Y'all making me feel real left out up here. Whispering and shit, leavin' me out of everything. I thought we were all in this together." She joked, but was serious.

Jahrome felt Babygirl grab on to him tighter. "Mami, like I said, when we get to where we're going, I got you. My sister's just going through it right now, and she needs me. I got you. Don't worry."

Ghost

Chapter 12

"That's 500 thousand, ma nigga. Now that you got yo' bread, how bout you put one of them packs up here and let me test my shit?" Jock said, looking the Haitian up and down with a slight mug.

He really didn't like fucking with his father's side of the family because all of them were arrogant assholes, but they had the best heroin. Most fiends drove all the way to Bankhead just to get his dope, and he had to make sure it was raw and uncut.

Marvey mugged his nephew for a long time. He was an evil man. His skin was blacker than ink, and he always looked angry. Had Jock not been his brother's son, he would have put a hot one in his head with no hesitation. He nodded his head, and one of his homies brought a duffel bag to the table. He pointed inside of it, eyeing Jock the whole time.

"Here's ya work right here, boy. Ya check ya tone when ya speak to me. Respect me like I respect you." He took a pull from the cocaine and weed-filled blunt, inhaling deeply, and eyeing Jock closely.

Jock walked over to the table with Gunz, surveying the room. There were four, heavily armed, masked soldiers from Bankhead whom Jock had personally chosen to be there.

The Haitians were only three deep, but they held DSK fully automatic weapons in their hands. Their eyes were bloodshot red.

Jock took his pocket knife out and stabbed the kilo of heroin, pulling out some and tested it. The feeling hit him right away. His body felt numb almost instantly, and then he felt free of pain and worry. It felt like his brain was having one orgasm after the next. He shook his head, and pulled the tape back over it. "On the strength that this is some good ass dope, and you hitting me for the low, I'm gon' let that last comment slide." He dropped 1 kilo into the bag, and zipped it up before standing up and facing Marvey. "But I'm just gon' let it pass this time. Next time, we gon' have a problem."

Marvey mugged him for a long time in silence with blood shot eyes. He almost looked sick. His long dreads were nappy. His clothes were wrinkled. Jock could smell his body odor.

"I gots ma money, and I'll see you when you're ready to re-up. Until then, count your blessings. But more importantly, count your breaths. You never know when you'll run out."

Jock watched them file out of the basement, and the man's last comments played over and over in his head, before he waved him off.

"Look, I want this shit busted down, and out to the traps by the morning. Time is muthafucking money, and the first of the month is upon us. We gotta hit the ground running."

He was ready to get his chips up before he fucked over Atlanta on behalf of his brother. He felt like he had been given some good intel in regards to his murder, and after he hustled for at least a week, he planned on torturing a few people.

* * *

Rico closed all of the blinds in his grandmother's house, and walked back into the living room with the AK-47 on the side of him. He was doped up on coke, and ready to have some shit pop off.

He handed the assault rifle to Jahrome. "This is your papa. This mafucka shoots 100 rounds. I got that stock enhancer on there, and it makes it spit rapidly. I'm tired of these mafuckas coming at me, bro. I know who it is. I told you we was gon' have a bunch of heat coming from the Cobras and the Asian

Bloods. That's a lot to deal with, but I'm a King, bro. I was made for this shit."

He sat at the table and made a thick line of cocaine before tooting it hard. It hit the back of his throat so hard that he coughed, before leaning his head down and tooting it into the other nostril. "Whoooo-weee! I'm ready to die! I'm ready to die! Are you ready, Jahrome?"

Jahrome looked at him like he was out of his mind. He didn't fuck with dope like that because it gave false confidence. Rico was talking about he was ready to die, and had already been hit more than ten times. He didn't know he could be speaking his own death into existence.

"Yo, all that shit sounds good, but hell naw. I ain't ready to die, nigga. If I go, who gon' make sure my mother and sister straight?"

"Santa Maria will, fool. We can't stop it from happening. When it's time to go, it's time to go, bro." He leaned down and tooted more of the powder.

One of his King homies, Placko, came from the back of the house carrying a MAC-10. He had on a gold shirt and black shorts, with matching Airmax shoes. He was skinny, shorts hanging off his ass and looked like he had seen better days.

"Say, Papa, I'm ready to kill some Asians, man. They're having a huge picnic at Garvey Park in one hour to celebrate Vuu-Wan coming home. Everybody's going to be there. It's the perfect time to fuck them over. I got the Kings in the basement ready to murder. We fucking wit' that angel dust."

Placko nodded at Jahrome. "What's good wit' you, fool? You rolling out wit' the family, or what?"

Jahrome lowered his head and shook it. He was feeling indecisive. He had a bad feeling about going with them niggas.

They were all doped up, and out of their minds. He didn't take them to be the smartest of killers.

Rico took a huge swallow of Hornitos after snorting another line. He staggered back and forth on his feet. "You ride wit' us tonight, Jahrome, and you're family. You're our fucking blood. My sister already is crazy about you, fool. I don't know what it is, but maybe you'll show me tonight."

He looked like he was about to fall over. Jahrome didn't have any faith in them. He felt like telling Rico something came up and he wouldn't be able to ride out with them. He had his sister and Mami heavily on his mind.

"Yeah, bro, you ride out, and you got family for life. Anything you need, you got it." Placko said, making a line so he could toot it up.

Against his better judgement, Jahrome decided he would fuck with them. He had a bad feeling something was going to happen.

* * *

Mami sat the plates into the sink and moved to the side so Babygirl could help her load them into the dishwasher. They had just finished some lasagna, and both women were full and missing Jahrome.

Babygirl stuck her hand into the water, and grabbed a plate, wiping it down with the soapy towel. "How long you think my brother gon' be with Rico? It's already after midnight." She said, fearing the worst. She missed him so bad. She needed for him to wrap his arms around her and tell her everything was going to be okay.

Mami took the plate from her and loaded it in the dishwasher. She felt like she should have been the first one to bring up Jahrome, but once again, Babygirl had beat her to the punch. "I don't know, but hopefully, it's soon. I'm worried about him, too. I'm not going to be able to sleep until he gets back here." She said, feeling low.

Babygirl felt a pain in her heart at hearing her respond in that way. She felt jealous. "Well, if you do fall asleep, I'll just wake you when he gets here." She lied.

When he made it home, she was going to find a way to hog him. There was only one extra bedroom, and she was sleeping on the couch in the living room. She would be the first person he saw when he came home, and if it was up to her, she wouldn't allow him to make it to the back room where Mami slept.

Mami frowned. "Can I ask you something, Babygirl?" She continued to load the dishwasher.

She already had an idea of what Mami was going to ask, but she wanted to hear it anyway.

"Yeah, you can ask me anything."

"Do you think since your accident, it's caused you to depend on your brother a little too much? It's almost like he's forced to cater to you every second of every day. I'm starting to get jealous." She looked up at her with serious eyes.

Babygirl scrunched her face, annoyed. "I don't know why you're feeling like that, because as long as I've been alive, my brother has been catering to me, and I've always been first in his life. That'll never change, and it shouldn't, not just because you came along." She rolled her eyes. "Far as my accident goes, yes, I think it's made me depend on him more, but that's just because all of the rest of the men in this world are trifling. My brother is not. He's a good man, and I'm supposed to feel safe with him, and I do."

Mami stood back and dried her hands on the yellow drying towel. She was getting more irritated. "I ain't mean for you to get all mad and shit. What I'm trying to say is I love your brother, even though we haven't been together for that long. I see the kind of man that he is, and I know for a fact I can hold him down one hundred percent. Now I'm not trying to come in between what y'all got going on, but I am a very jealous female. I like to have my man all to myself. I don't like sharing, but I feel like I have to make an exception because of who you are to him. But honestly, I don't like it. It's making me feel some type of way, *mamita*."

I don't want to share him with you either bitch, Babygirl thought. She really wanted to expose her true feelings about her brother, but she just couldn't bring herself say it out loud.

Instead, she kept her thoughts to herself. She didn't want to be vulnerable to Mami. Babygirl already had countless reasons Jahrome would ultimately choose her and only her.

"Mami, I think my brother really does care about you, and that makes me happy because you and I have always been cool. I think you're a good woman. And I know you'll hold him down. Right now, I'm just going through some battles, but I'll be stronger soon, and you'll have him all to yourself, I promise." She said, feeling sick to her stomach imagining that.

Every word she said made her hate Mami that much more, with her long, natural curly hair, and her flawless face with the baby hair along the edges. She hated her C-cup titties, and her perfectly portioned body. She even hated her perfect little toes that were always done. The bitch was too bad in her eyes. She had felt that way ever since she'd laid eyes on her at the club. Mami always made Babygirl feel like she had to compete.

Had she let down her guard, she knew for a fact her brother would fall in love with Mami easily, and then he would forget all about her. Then who would want her? Who would want a woman with a long scar across her face who was emotionally damaged? She blinked back tears. The relationship with

Reggie coupled with the abused she'd been subjected to as a child, had really messed her up.

Mami put her arm around her shoulder. "Aww, thank you, girl. I was worried you didn't even like me because I was with your brother. But you know I did come to you first, unlike that bitch, Star. She fucked your brother without even coming to you like a woman."

Mami could only imagine what she was going through, but she felt it was her duty to be there for her as much as possible whenever Jahrome wasn't around. Maybe if she healed her as much as she could before he got there, he wouldn't have so much work to do.

"I think I just need to lie down." She was about to make her way to the couch when Mami led her in the direction of the bedroom. "Naw, girl, come on and lay in the bed. That way, you can stretch all the way out. I'll wait up for Jahrome. I'm finna hit his phone in a minute to see where he is, and how long it's going to take him to get back here."

Ghost

Chapter 13

"You see, that's what I'm saying, papa, I don't know why everybody thinks it's cool to park a block down from the park on Robinson Street whenever they have their cookouts and celebrations. To me, it's a death trap because now they have to walk a whole ass block to link back up with all of their homies. That's just stupid and makes it easy for us to knock them off group by group." Rico said, slamming the long magazine into his MAK-90, watching Jahrome do the same to his fully automatic as he sat across from him in the passenger seat of his Jeep Grand Cherokee, or as Rico calls it, his "Hit 'Em Up Mobile."

Jahrome grunted and glared at Rico. "Most of these niggas probably don't think things through, and therein lies the problem." Jahrome smirked. "I mean, for them, anyway."

Rico sniffed hard. He could taste the residue of the Peruvian flake in the back of his throat. He was high as a kite, and ready to jump off into some action. "Say, *ese*, these muthafuckin' Asians gotta get what's coming to them. The muthafuckas' names are Alli and Tommy. Both are scumbags, and I'ma make sure at least one, if not both, of them eat more than a few of my slugs. I wanna move these *vatos* around, and then, we can take a good look at these fuckin' snakes. You feel me?"

Jahrome nodded. He honestly didn't give a fuck about Rico's wars. He was just thinking he needed to do whatever it took to keep Rico in his corner until he was able to move away from Georgia. The bottom line was he needed his protection and partnership. Both were beneficial in their survival. "I feel you, mane. Now, let's go peel these muthafuckas' tops back."

Rico looked into the back seat at two of his security men. "Y'all good back there?" He asked them in Spanish. Both men nodded and cocked their weapons. They were bloodthirsty and ready to get things moving. Rico was paying them five G's a piece for the hits.

Rico looked back over to Jahrome. "Everybody is ready. We gon' let this sun set more, and then we finna go and handle this bidness."

"That sound good to me." Jahrome pulled a stuffed Garcia Vega from his pocket, and sparked the blunt. "I'ma roll for a minute until we ready to make this shit happen. It looks like it'll be dark in about thirty minutes to an hour."

Rico nodded his head. "That sounds good to me. Gon' head and roll around for a bit. I need to holler at you anyway on some other shit." Rico pulled the seatbelt across his chest.

"Say, mane, y'all click them seat belts in place so the Police won't be fuckin' wit' us." He ordered his shooters. Both men grumbled before clicking their seat belts in place.

Jahrome blew a cloud of smoke toward the ceiling of the truck, and looked over to Rico. "What's good, homeboy? You got something on your mind?" He lowered his window just a tad.

Rico laughed. "Aw, it's no big deal, just something that's been driving me crazy." He let his seat back, and tilted the steering wheel so he could slump against the driver's door. "I wanna know about Mami, and how you truly feel about her. You know, man to man."

Jahrome took three pulls, and inhaled hard. "You mean, you wanna talk about some emotional shit while we're about to be in the mist of bodying all of these Asian niggas. Didn't you say the Bloods were straight killas?"

Rico nodded. "So what? We are, too. Why does that make a difference?" Rico kept cruising. He rolled past the park, and saw their targets setting up for their party. The park was already packed with Asian bangers. Rico recognized more than a few of them. He laughed to himself when he laid eyes on Alli and Snake. Both men were embracing a few members from their crew.

Rico felt a chill go down his spine. Both men had been his enemies when he went to Caesar E. Chavez High School. He held hatred in his heart for both men.

"So, shoot, Rico, what do you really wanna know about Mami?" Jahrome didn't feel like explaining himself to another man, but at the same time, he couldn't afford to get into any disagreements with Rico. He felt the sooner he got the conversation over with, the better off he would be.

Rico shrugged his shoulders. "I just wanna know what your intentions are with her, *ese*. Like, do you really love her? Can you see yourself being with her for a long time?" Mami was Rico's heart, and in his mind, she was all he had in the cold world.

Jahrome shrugged his shoulders. "Bruh, I love her. She means a lot to me. We been through some major shit together, and through it all, we've held each other down. I don't know what tomorrow holds, but as of right now, she got my heart."

Jahrome couldn't help thinking about Babygirl as soon as he said anything about Mami having his heart. As much as he hated to admit it, nobody had his heart more than his sister.

Every time he found himself lost in a daze, he was thinking about her.

Rico bent another corner and smiled. "That's good to hear, Jahrome, because I fuck with you. I honestly think you really do care about my sister. As far as I can see, she's crazy about yo' ass, too. I've never heard or seen her talk about somebody to me as much as she does you. That's saying a lot, trust me."

Jahrome nodded. "That's what's up. I can only build off of that knowledge. Now, are you done grilling me? Can we get back to the task at hand?" Jahrome said this in a joking manner, but he meant it with every fiber of his being. He didn't want to sit around and talk about females and emotions when he needed to be in a murderous state of mind.

Rico laughed as the sun began to set. "Yeah, let's do that."

"How the fuck are we going to penetrate these muthafuckas enough to take out the main players you're looking to hit? Do we just bust and hit as many random enemies as possible?" He was worried Rico really didn't have a plan, and that spelled disaster in his brain.

Rico curled his lip, and mugged Jahrome. "Far as I'm concerned, as long as we hit as many as we can, that'll be perfectly fine wit' me. Like I said, if we can hit one or both of them two, that'll sweeten the pot even more." Rico knew multiple bodies meant business. He was looking to move the Asian crew around, and the only thing they responded to was bloodshed. It had been that way for as long as he could remember.

Jahrome shook his head and dumped the ashes from the blunt into the ashtray of the truck. "That shit sounds messy to me. If there's one thing I learned about the game, it's you just can't jump up and bust moves without thinking them all the way through. Calculation and premeditation prevents mistakes and losses. We're fuckin' with a whole crew of animals. It seems only right that we think shit through before we go at them."

"We ain't got no time for all of that. They usually make shit happen from behind closed doors. The fact they're actually going to be slipping at this park tonight is a blessing in disguise. We gotta capitalize off of this. Ain't no telling when we'll be able to catch them slipping in such a fashion again."

Jahrome didn't like how Rico was carrying on. He wanted to say so much, but in the end, he decided to keep his thoughts and comments to himself. Whatever the mission called for, he felt he would be able to roll with the punches. He was smart enough to make it out alive, and always had been. "Aiight, then, let's handle this bidness. I got other shit to do. I'm rolling wit' you."

Rico smiled. "That's what I'm talking about, *ese*. Just trust me. After this lick here, we'll be able to lay low for a minute. You and my sister can chill, and I can catch up on a few other things."

His phone buzzed. A text came through, letting him know the rest of his crew was ready to move on the Asian animals. Rico smiled. "Everybody's ready. The sun is down. Let's get it over with."

Jahrome sucked his teeth, and looked Rico over. "Yeah, let's do that."

***

An hour later, after meeting up with the rest of Rico's crew, Jahrome sat on the floor of the Chevy Astro van with his MAK-90 cocked and loaded. His heart beat fast in his chest. He had strange a feeling that something wasn't going to go right. He chopped the ill feeling up to nerves, and was forced to shrug it off as the van came to a halt. He jumped out of the side door next to Rico.

They were six houses from the park. Rico had ordered his hittas be dropped off all around the park so it could be hit from all angles. The Asian Bloods had all of the streets blocked off so no cars could get in or out of the park. This would make the ambush nearly impossible.

Jahrome and Rico took off jogging toward the get-together as soon as their feet hit the pavement in the alley. When they got two houses from the gathering, they could hear the loud music playing out of the speakers.

Rico looked across the way at the park and saw Tommy grooving in the open with a slender female in a short skirt. His hands were all over her ass. About twenty feet from him was Alli. He also had a female and appeared to be doing the same things to her.

Rico couldn't help cheesing under his mask. He picked up his walkie talkie and gave the orders for his men to attack.

He held his MAK-90 at shoulder length and ran from the side of the house directly across from the park, busting at Tommy and Alli, and his hittas followed suit. In a matter of seconds, the park sounded like fireworks on the Fourth of July.

Jahrome hesitated before running across the street. He was a bit annoyed by the stunt Rico just pulled. The man had took off running and gunning without making him aware of what he was going to do. He watched Rico splatter Tommy. He stood over the fallen man and popped five slugs into his face before chasing behind Alli.

The Asians returned fire. Jahrome watched a few of Rico's men get shot up and dropped. Then, the shooters were dropped in cold blood by a barrage of bullets from more of Rico's crew.

Heavy gun smoke was in the atmosphere. Women screamed and ran away from the park, and Jahrome could literally hear men hollering out in agony as bullets entered their bodies. He waited a full two minutes before he decided to enter the war zone.

Rico emptied his clip into Tommy's younger brother. He lost sight of Alli because of him. After smoking him, he backed up with a deranged look in his eyes. He looked around and saw fallen men everywhere. "Hell yeah!" He mused.

He was just about to take off running, when Alli flipped the picnic table and jumped up. He held two .40 calibers in his hand. He locked his sights on Rico, and bit into his bottom lip, before pulling the triggers. "Muthafucka!"

Jahrome ran and aimed, bussing his MAK-90 back to back. His first bullets ripping into Alli's temple, flipping the man around. By the time Jahrome got closer to him, and finished him off, Rico had already jumped up and took off running.

Ghost

Chapter 14

"Seems like every time I see you, you're always looking so down. I don't like that." Gunz said as he placed the grocery bags into the back of Dymond's Benz truck.

It was his duty to be on security for her whenever she got close to the city of Atlanta. His orders were shoot to kill if anything looked fishy.

As he placed the last bag into the car, he looked around and scanned the area of the grocery store parking lot. Everything looked normal. It was just starting to rain, and there were only a few people around.

Dymond sat in the driver's seat and closed the door, lowering her head. She was so depressed. She didn't know what to do. It didn't matter how much money Jock spent on her or their daughter. It wasn't enough to make her happy. She felt alone and afraid. She was afraid of Jock. Afraid that one day, she would be targeted for the sins he committed.

Gunz got into the passenger's seat, just as the rain started to come down heavily. His heart was heavy for her. Deep in his heart, he had a soft spot for her. When they were in the fifth grade, they had been boyfriend and girlfriend, and even though that was old news, his feelings for her never dissipated. Even though she had got with Jock, they did absolutely nothing to change how he felt. Although he felt as though Jock didn't deserve her, he stayed in his own lane.

He reached over and rubbed her soft cheek. "Talk to me, beautiful. I'm here to listen."

Dymond looked over at him, shocked. She couldn't believe he had enough balls to touch her. He wasn't afraid of what Jock would do to him, and she knew personally if Jock had known, he would have cut him up into little bitty pieces, and would probably force her to eat him with a fork.

She felt vulnerable. She lowered her head, and put her face into her hands, crying her heart out. Gunz rubbed her back. He shook his head, while continuing to scan the area of the parking lot. The rain was coming down so hard.

"Talk to me, Dymond. It's okay. Tell me what's the matter."

She shook her head, and lifted it enough to show him her wet face. "I'm so depressed. I'm tired of this life. I'm tired of being in a relationship with a man who doesn't even love me. All he cares about is Aerial. The only time he shows me any real affection is while we're in front of her, but as soon as she walks away, he's cold to me. He never tells me he loves me, and the only time he touches me is to discipline me. There is no lovemaking. I don't know when we last went out and had a romantic dinner. Being a kingpin's wife isn't all it's cracked up to be. This life sucks. I feel trapped." She whimpered and buried her face back into her hands.

She didn't know why she was admitting all of these things to him, but she just couldn't stop talking. For some reason, she felt safe and as though

she could trust him.

Gunz continued to rub her back, and pulled her over to him, picking her up and sitting her on his lap after letting the seat back a little bit. He knew he was taking a risk. He knew if Jock found out, his life would be over, but he didn't care. He cared about her, and to him, she was worth the risk.

Dymond felt like a little girl being picked up by her father. She was about to be consoled by a man who actually cared. So before he even spoke, she placed her face into his neck, and inhaled his cologne, then her tears started up again.

Gunz rubbed her back. She smelled so good to him and felt soft. He wrapped her into his big arms and held her.

"Dymond, you already know that's my mans right there, and I been riding with the homie ever since we were kids. I don't agree with a lot of the things he does, but it's because of him that I'm eating, so I honor him. However, I've been crazy about you ever since the fifth grade, and one of the reasons I have been so close to him is because of you. I had to make sure you're protected at all times, because you're special."

Dymond sat up, and looked into his chubby face, rubbing it with her thumb. "Are you serious? You really think I'm special?" Her heart started to beat super fast. She had not heard a man tell her she was special since she was five years old, and a teacher had told her that in the first grade. No man had ever told her that, so hearing it from Gunz was making her weak.

"Please tell me more, Gunz. I need to hear it. I just need to hear a man cater to my emotions for once because I'm so lost. I need to hear it so bad." She said with her voice breaking up. Her throat felt like it hurt. Her body began to shake in anticipation of the words that were about to come out of his mouth. She kissed him on the cheek, and placed her face back into his neck, wiggling her bottom in his lap almost enticingly, but sex was the furthest thing from her mind. Her emotions needed repair.

Gunz held her tighter and kissed her cheek. He rubbed her head, and held her like a little girl. "Dymond, you are really special, and you are strong. You should never allow any man, or anybody, to dictate how to feel about you. You are an incredible woman. You're beautiful, and you have to realize pain don't last forever. It fades, and then, the true you will blossom into greatness, because that's what you are. Regardless of what Jock tells you, you are a phenomenal woman."

He kissed her again. He felt like he was betraying Jock. Jock had always been loyal to him. Out of all the niggas in their crew, Jock let him do him, and rarely ever came down on him about anything. He helped him to get hood rich, just like him. However, the quest for Dymond's love and comfort outweighed his street morals.

Dymond kissed his neck, and then kissed his cheek, taking his face into her hands. She held it steady, looking him in the eyes for a long time.

"Gunz, I need you. I need you to be here for me. I need you to be my escape. Niggas think they can throw money and gifts at a woman, and that's all it takes to keep them happy, but that is so far from the truth. We need more than that. We need more than gold. We are emotional beings. You sitting here and holding me, and telling me these things, it's like these ten minutes are worth more than two weeks of shopping."

Gunz took a deep breath and nodded. When she leaned in to kiss his lips, every part of him wanted to prevent it from happening, but he couldn't. He always had a yearning for her that never went away.

* * *

Jahrome stepped on to the porch, looking over his shoulder, paranoid, hoping that he had not been followed. He knew he shouldn't have been fucking around with Rico. Now there were a whole bunch of people dead, and if not for Jahrome, Rico could have been one of them. He shook his head and adjusted the gun on his waist. He stepped forward to knock on the door, but the porch light came on, and Mami opened the door, wrapping her arms around his neck. "*Papi*, I missed you so much. I been in here going crazy worrying about you."

She kissed his juicy lips, before sucking all over them, and pressing her pelvis into him, moaning in his mouth. Jahrome picked her up, and closed the door, making sure it was locked all the way. Even though he was still paranoid, there was nothing like having a bad woman greet you at the door, yearning.

"I been out here fucking wit' yo' crazy ass brother. That nigga almost got us killed, but we good." He heard a car roll past outside and the hairs on the back of his neck stood up.

Mami sucked on his neck hard before biting into it. She wanted him bad. She had been fiending for him for a few days. "Baby, I'm just glad you're okay. I need you right now. I want you to take me right here in this living room. Please." She dropped to her knees, rubbing his crotch, locating his thick piece and squeezing it into her small hand. "Ummm, I want some of this."

Jahrome took his pistols and threw them on the couch, looking down on her as she opened his fly, pulling his dick out. She kissed the head before sucking it into her mouth, and going to town on it loudly. His toes curled immediately. Her mouth felt like a hot fist stroking him. He grabbed her curly hair, as his eyes rolled back into his head.

Babygirl crept down the hall, and stopped in the dining room, and watched Jahrome hump into Mami's mouth. She felt jealous and turned on at the same time. As she stood there, she rubbed her thighs together, feeling her juices pool between her thighs. She moaned deep within her throat.

Mami stroked his dick up and down, looking him in the eyes. "You're a little sweaty, *papi*, but it's good. This is how I show you that I love you." She started bobbing her head on his dick at full speed, sucking loudly, stroking him with her hand. She stopped and pulled up her tank top, exposing her brown titties, then bent over the couch.

"Fuck me, *papi*. Please fuck me right here, as hard as you can because I need you." She pulled her pink Victoria Secret panties down, and bent back over, spreading her lips with two fingers so he could see her little pink hole. It glistened with her juices, inviting him.

Jahrome stepped forward with his piece and smacked it on her heavy ass cheeks. He still couldn't believe how thick she was. He had run across a lot of Spanish women, and by far, Mami was the finest.

He pressed forward and slowly slid into her hotness. It felt like he was putting his dick into a tight glove. As soon as he got all the way in, her walls started to milk him. He grabbed her hips and slammed her into him.

"Uh! Uh! Uh! Uh! *Papi*, yes! Uh! Fuck me, *papi*! Please do me harder." She moaned, bouncing back into him with her titties bouncing against her stomach. His dick stretched her open. She could feel him in her lower abdomen, and it made her feel whole. The fact that Jahrome made her feel stuffed was enough to drive her crazy.

He grabbed her hips and slammed into her again and again, fucking that pussy the way it was supposed to be fucked. Her juices dripped off his balls, and on to the carpet. She had that good box, the kind men bragged about. Every time he pulled back, he slammed back into her with power. It sounded like somebody was in the room clapping their hands together repeatedly. It didn't take long for their scent to permeate the air.

Mami reached back and spread herself wider for him. She wanted to make sure he went as deep into her as he could go.

That was the great thing about having a man with a huge dick. He grabbed a handful of her hair, and yanked her head backward.

124

"Uhh, shit, yes, *papi*, treat my ass! I love how you be doing me. Do me, *papi*!" She smashed her ass back into his lap. The more he treated her like he didn't care while he fucked her, the wetter she got. She felt the orgasm building, getting stronger and stronger. Her body started to shake and vibrate. She gripped a pillow on the couch and tilted her head back as he continued to fuck her harder and harder from the back.

She couldn't take it anymore. It felt too good, and he was taking her breath away. She lost the battle and let go. "Ahhhh! Sheeeiiittt! *Papiiii!*" Her body started shaking harder.

Babygirl squatted down with both of her fingers in her pussy going in and out of her. Her juices leaked down her wrist, and her nipples were so hard that they hurt. She watched his dick slam in and out of her pussy. She took in the sounds, the smell, and the way he was destroying her. It was all too much. She started to come when he pulled all the way back and she saw his dick glistening in the lamp light.

Jahrome stepped on to his toes and slammed three hard times and came deep in Mami's pussy. Jerk after jerk, it sent his body into a frenzy. Mami's walls sucked at him as if they were begging for his nut. As soon as he pulled out of her, he was exhausted. She turned around and dropped in front of him, sucking her juices off of him hungrily.

As they made their to the bedroom, they'd discovered Babygirl under the covers appearing to be sleep in their king sized bed. Mami noted this, and she felt a little down, but she was too tired to put up a fight.

"Should we wake her up?" She asked him, completely worn all the way out. She had been up for nearly two days straight stressing over him.

Jahrome took off his shirt, exposing his rock hard body, before stripping down to his boxers. He was ready to call it a night. He didn't care where his sister slept, just as long as everybody went to sleep. He crawled into the bed and laid down in the middle. "Let's just get some sleep, baby. You already know morning will be here before you know it. And then, we only gon' have one day before you gotta go to Miami and get that money, so I wanna spend the whole day with you if I can."

Mami nodded, and slowly laid down, snuggling up to him with her back to his chest. She could feel his long pipe lined up against her ass, and it made her smile. She wiggled her butt a little bit until she got comfortable enough to fall out.

* * *

Jahrome had been sleeping for about an hour when he felt a hand go inside of his boxer hole and pull his dick out. For a second, he just laid there with his eyes closed. His brain didn't fully process what was going on. He felt himself being stroked, and then he felt heat, sucking at him with force. He moaned deep within his throat and humped his hips forward. He could hear Mami lightly snoring to his left.

At the realization of that, it caused his eyes to pop open, just as the mouth sucked harder.

"It's my turn now, Jahrome. I need you. I want you to do me just like you did her. Please." She scooted beside him with her back to him and humped into him again and felt his head go past her lips, almost penetrating her hole.

Jahrome put his hand between them, pulling his piece away from her. "Sis, we can't do that. Come on now. You know I love you, but you're just vulnerable right now." He held his breath to see if he could still hear Mami breathing normally. Being that she hadn't gotten any sleep within the past two days, she seemed to be in a deep slumber.

126

Babygirl bit into his neck and sucked on it. She pulled her hips forward, making his dick go into her again, before he pulled out again. "Please, I need it so bad. Why won't you fuck me, Jahrome? I don't care what nobody thinks. I love you, and I should have you in every way. Please don't deny me." She whimpered, and tried to put him all the way inside. His dick head sat on her wet lips, before dropping to her thick thighs. She picked it up and tried again, opening her lips with two fingers.

Jahrome was in a battle between good and evil. He knew what she was proposing wasn't right. But at the same time, he knew she needed him. He loved his sister with all of him, and there was nothing he wouldn't do for her. He just only wished she didn't need that part of him, and it hurt his heart to deny her.

Babygirl sucked his earlobe, squeezing his big dick in her hand. "I need this, Jahrome. I'm hurting so bad right now, and you're the only one who can heal me. I'll do anything for this right here." She lifted her leg, and placed it on his waist, scooting forward. His head slowly went past her lips. Her kitty tingled in anticipation. She couldn't wait to finally feel him inside of her. She needed him now more than ever.

Jahrome felt himself penetrating her wetness. He thought about pulling back, but then he saw the tears in her eyes, and all of his defenses were lowered. He gave in and allowed her to slowly guide him inside.

Mami woke up screaming. "Ahh! Ahh! Help me! Help me! Help me!" She screamed, and sat up in bed.

That caused both of them to nearly jump out of their skin. Jahrome pulled his dick out immediately, turned around and wrapped her into his arms. "Baby, baby, wake up. You're dreaming." He said, gently shaking her until her eyes opened.

Babygirl slowly slipped from the bed, defeated. She walked out of the room, only stopping once to look back at her brother, and the way he consoled Mami. It broke her heart all over again. She wanted to get rid of her. She had to find a way.

Jahrome watched her walk out of the room with his heart beating fast in his chest. He wanted to get up and follow her to make sure she was okay.

Chapter 15

Linda just got out of church, and she was getting ready to show the sisters how she got down in the kitchen. They took turns inviting the elder members of the church to their homes each Sunday, and this was her week. Her and all of the sisters had arrived at her house, and were standing at her door. The thunder boomed behind her, and the rain started to come down full force.

"Sister, I promise you gon' love my peach cobbler. When I throw down, I throw down. Hold my purse for a second, so I can open it and fish my keys out." She said, handing the big purse to Sister Robinson.

"Chile, will you find them keys? You're getting me and Sister Patterson all wet." Sister Robinson said, holding the purse. She had been hesitant about coming to Linda's home because the neighborhood in which Linda resided looked a bit suspect.

"Gal, hold your horses. Now I just about got 'em if you give me a second."

"In a second, you gon' ruin my best Sunday hat. Hurry up!" Sister Patterson said, getting annoyed by the minute.

Linda found the keys, and unlocked the door. As soon as they made it inside, they stomped their feet on her welcome mat before taking their coats off and hanging them on a hook.

Linda's place was warm and cozy. She had left Kirk Franklin playing on the radio, and the smell of her sweet home cooking was fresh in the air.

"Would you sistas like anything to drink while I get the food ready?" She said, setting her Bible on the glass table.

Jock stepped out of the kitchen with a .44 Desert Eagle in his hand. He aimed it right at her forehead, before Gunz stepped out of the kitchen behind him. "Now, I think that's kind of rude you would ask them if they wanted anything, but leave me and the homie out."

He stepped forward and grabbed her by the throat. "Bitch, where are yo' kids? Did yo' punk ass son kill my brother?"

Sister Patterson's eyes got big as saucers before she fainted. She still had her Bible in her hand.

Sister Robinson peed a little in her Depends. She didn't know what was going on, but she was scared for her life. She knew she made the wrong decision by coming to Sister Linda's house. She stayed in a seedy part of Atlanta, which gave her the creeps. She didn't know how the woman had survived as long as she had without getting shot. She shook her head, before throwing her hands in the air.

Jock tightened his grip on Linda.

"Did you hear what the fuck I asked you?" He asked through clenched teeth.

Linda kept her mouth shut and didn't make eye contact with him. In her mind, he wasn't nothing but the devil, and she didn't fear the devil. He could take her physically, but she would be with her spiritual father at the end of the day.

"Young man, how about you take your hands off me, and get out of my house."

Jock turned his head to the side and nodded. "Aw, you've got some heart, old lady, huh?" He looked over to Gunz, and smiled, before curling his lip in disgust. He picked her up by her throat, lifting her into the air, before slamming her down through the glass table with all of his might.

Glass shot up into the air. Sister Robinson smacked her hands to her cheeks and let out a loud scream, before Gunz stepped forward and punched her so hard that she flew into the wall and spit her dentures out. They rolled under the couch, and she fell with her head between her legs, knocked out cold.

Linda struggled to get up. Glass dropped off of her, and on to the carpet. She felt weak and dizzy. She struggled to breathe. Then, he lifted her again into the air, and threw her down to the floor. This time, the impact knocked the wind out of her, and her hip snapped. The intense pain shot from her hip to her back.

Jock wiped his mouth with his black gloves. All he cared about was getting revenge and making a statement. All the fingers pointed to their family. Nothing else made sense to him, so if he had to torture some information out of the old woman, so be it. He leaned down and pulled out his scalpel, grabbing a handful of her hair, until her wig came off.

He threw it across the room, and frowned. He grabbed her nappy hair into his fist, and he sliced her across the face with the blade twice. Blood oozed down, and dripped off her chin.

"Where the fuck yo' kids at, bitch?" Linda started to scream as the blade sliced into her face, stinging her. She felt blood run into her eye, and she began to shake out of fear.

"Ahhh! I don't know where they are. I don't know what happened to your brother. I don't even know who your brother is." She lied as she cried.

Jock loved when his victims cried. It made him feel powerful. He sliced her across the face repeatedly, loving the way the skin peeled away, showing him her inner pink before it bled. He sliced her over and over again.

"Did yo' son kill my brother? Did yo' son kill my brother and take my dope? Tell me something, old lady, because my arm ain't gon' get tired." He continued to slice her face.

Sister Robinson prayed to God that she wasn't his next victim.

Linda's face was mangled. She knew Jock was going to kill her anyway. She wasn't going to assist the killer in hurting her babies, so she was ready to go to the grave with what she knew.

Gunz was feeling uneasy about how Jock was doing the old woman. He felt it was all unnecessary. He wished he would have just killed her and got it over with. He started to imagine the woman being his mother and it made him feel even more sick on the stomach.

Jock picked her up and threw her into the china cabinet, shattering it. Big shards poked into her face and neck. Blood ran from her nose and into her mouth, nearly choking her.

He walked over and sliced her across the face again, imagining she was his grandmother who used to beat him when he was little. She used to beat him until he bled for the pettiest of things.

Linda stumbled forward, reaching for the air. She felt weak, blanking in and out. The world seemed darker. She imagined the face of her daughter when she was first born, and the last sight of her in the hospital. Then, she thought about Jahrome, as a little boy, with his dimples and hazel eyes. Then, she saw how he looked the last time she saw him. Her heart started to hurt, and then, there was a sharp, stinging pain that shot up her left arm that paralyzed her and caused her to fall on to her face

Jock knelt down while Linda shook, took her head, and slammed it into the floor with all of his might, busting it open. He hated her for dying on him. He just knew she was strong enough to tolerate the pain he had subjected her to. Hated her for leaving before she admitted to anything. Hated her for giving birth to children who were possibly responsible for killing his brother.

He jumped up and walked to Sister Robinson, smacking her awake.

Her eyes opened and she immediately started crying. "Oh, please, don't hurt me, baby. I don't know anything."

Jock pulled her up by her throat and looked her deep in the eyes. "That bitch didn't tell you nothing about where her kids could be?"

She shook her head hard. "I swear before God she didn't. If she had told me anything, I would have told you already." She crossed her finger across her chest in the sign of a crucifix.

He shook his head in anger. "Gunz, kill this bitch, and that one, too. I want you to snap their necks. Now!" He ordered, standing up and dusting off his Tom Ford pants.

Gunz felt sick to his stomach, but he knew he had to follow Jock's orders. He silently asked God to forgive him, and prayed nothing happened to his mother because of what he was about to do.The sound of her neck snapping was so loud, Jock hunched his shoulders. She fell to the floor with her chin facing her back.

Gunz picked up Sister Patterson, and threw her against the wall, choking her with two hands. He squeezed with all of his might, and then punched her in her chest. She took a deep breath, and he tightened his grip on her neck.

She felt her lungs burst, and then her chest filled up with blood. The explosion caused her heart to pause, beat, and then pause again, enough to make her go limp. Blood vessels burst in her eyes, and then she was shaking like crazy. Jock watched her face turn blue, and her eyes roll into the back of her head.

Gunz dropped her and stepped over her. "Where are we off to next?"

* * *

Click! Click! "Wake up, *papi!* Wake up, *papi,* please!" Mariella screamed, looking down at Rico. She had tears in her eyes and a shotgun to the back of her head. She not only feared for her life, but for the life of her daughter. Rico had shown up at her house drunk, trying to get her to have sex with him.

Rico slowly opened his eyes and felt the hangover. He felt like throwing up. As his vision slowly cleared, he made out his baby mother pointing his .45 at him. There were tears streaming down her cheeks, and her mascara ran and dripped off of her chin.

He tried to sit up, but she pressed the barrel to his forehead. "Don't move, *papi*. I swear to god I'll shoot you, because they have our daughter, and they told me if I don't kill you, they're going to kill her."

She jerked the gun, and spoke through clenched teeth. "Now, I can't let that happen, so you better tell them what they need to know so we can make it out of here, and I can get her back. You got it?" She frowned, her face full of hatred.

Behind her, the short masked man poked her harder in the head with the shotgun. "Where does that nigger live who helped you kill my homeboys at the picnic?"

Rico felt his heartbeat speed up. He looked down at his chest and noticed he didn't have his bulletproof vest on. He felt unprotected and vulnerable.

He went to flight mode. "Bra, that shit ain't have nothing to do wit' me, papa. I ain't wanna move on you fools, but he insisted. I don't like all this drama shit, homeboy! I was ready to sit down and form a treaty with your Blood homies, but he wasn't having that. Once he started shooting, my niggas followed suit and shit happened!" He lied, and felt his stomach turn upside down.

Mariella couldn't believe how Rico bitched up and outed one of his homeboys. Her brother, Ramón, had died keeping his mouth closed. To her, he had been a real man. Rico in her eyes was a pure bitch.

The masked man cocked the shotgun and pointed it at Rico. "I said, where does he live, fool? Where that nigger from? I ain't gon' ask you again."

Rico replied, "His mother got a crib over on Western in Atlanta, but right now, he's staying with my sister at her crib. I don't care what you do to him, but please leave my sister out of it. She's innocent in all of this." He said, feeling like a pussy for even putting her under the gun. He was bogus and he knew it.

The masked man nodded. "You think I'm gon' believe you ain't have nothin' to do with my homies getting killed? Huh? What you take me for, fool?" He yanked the gun out of Mariella's hand and popped it on safety, turning it upside down. "I want you to take this gun and beat this fool's head in until I tell you to stop. You understand me?" He growled.

Mariella straddled Rico and took the gun from the masked man. "I gotta do what I gotta do, Rico. This is your fault. You brought this drama to my home. All because your drunk ass wanted some pussy when you know I'm with Hector." She raised the gun and looked over her shoulder at Tango. "Should I do it now?"

The masked man curled his lip. He was second in command of the Asian Bloods and had lost three of his cousins because of Rico and his crew. He hated the Puerto Rican and everyone who looked like him.

He nodded. "Crash him, and I'll tell you when to stop."

Rico closed his eyes and got ready for the impact. He hoped Mariella didn't hit hard.

"You know what, Rico, you ain't nothing but a dog, *papi!*" She slammed the gun into his head with all of her might. *Wham!* The handle of the gun connected with his forehead, and vibrated in her hands.

She lifted the gun and brought it down again. *Wham!* Rico kicked his legs as he felt the impact of the assault. It felt like he had been hit in the head with a shovel, and each blow after that hurt worse. Blood seeped into his right eye.

Mariella had her tongue hanging out of her mouth, entranced in the action. She brought the pistol down again and again, and busted his head wide open. She thought about all of the times he had forced himself on her, and all of the times he beat her in front of their daughter. All of the times he said he was going to show up and didn't, and all of the times she had to hold her daughter at night while she cried herself to sleep over missing him.

Bam! Bam! Bam! "You're full of shit, Rico! You ain't nothing but a fucking liar!" She screamed, beating him senselessly.

Rico was far gone. He saw her swinging the gun down, but he felt nothing. The pain had already subsided, and he was on his way to another place. His vision got dark.

Mariella beat him until his face was basically mush. He looked like a smashed pumpkin two weeks after Halloween.

The masked man smiled and slammed the shotgun to the back of her head. *Booom! Booom!* She was dead before she even knew the gun went off. Tango pushed her on the floor, and put the shotgun into Rico's mouth and pulled the trigger. *Booom!*

Chapter 16

Gunz and Dymond were parked in the back of the Boys & Girls Club of Buckhead. Aerial went to the club every day after school because the place had tutors who helped her with her homework. It had been about two weeks since the last they saw each other.

"How are you feeling, baby?" Gunz asked before kissing Dymond on her juicy lips. She sucked all over his lips and laid her head on his shoulder. The hadn't placed a label on who they were to one another, they just simple enjoyed one another's company.

"I'm feeling good, baby, just as long as you have some kind words for me." She joked, sitting back in her seat, clasping her fingers with his.

Gunz looked around and made sure they weren't being watched. He always felt a little apprenensive about being alone with her now. He knew sooner or later, Jock would find out, and he didn't even want to imagine what that looked like. Quiet as kept, he was falling hard for her.

"Baby, I missed you, and I be thinking about you all the time. I wish I could take you away from the homie, and make it so that you never have to go through any of the pains that you feel on a daily basis ever again. I'd give you the world every single day, 'cause you deserve it."

Dymond felt her heart flutter. Every word he spoke made her fall for him more. She wanted be with Gunz. She needed to be. "Gunz, I wanna tell you something, but I don't want you to freak out." She looked into eyes more serious this time.

He leaned into her and kissed her juicy lips. "You can tell me anything, baby. Anything that's on your heart, I need to hear it."

"I wanna run away with you. I want us to leave Atlanta, and go as far away from here as possible. I need you more than I ever thought I would. I'm sick, and it seems like you're the only one who understands what I'm going through, and how to be there for me."

She looked up at him, afraid of his response. She was hoping she wasn't coming on too strong.

"Baby, are you mad at me for thinking like that?"

Gunz was quiet for a long time. He was trying to figure out what he should do. He was extremely loyal to Jock, so a part of him wanted to have his cake and eat it, too. As crazy at leaving Atlanta may have seemed, he was down for it.

"Baby, are you going to say something?" Dymond asked, worried. *Damn, I probably said too much*, she thought. "You know what, it's cool. I was just thinking out loud. I mean, we don't have to do anything like that right away. Maybe down the line somewhere, you know, if we're still feeling the way we're feeling." She kissed his cheek and nuzzled her face into his thick neck.

"What about Aerial? Are you thinking about taking her along, and if so, how would we do that? You know bruh would have the whole world looking for our asses."

He held her more tightly and looked into her pretty brown eyes. Dymond felt giddy all over. She couldn't believe he was actually considering leaving with her. It made her feel special.

She took a deep breath. "Okay, so what I was thinking, I wanted to take my daughter with us, but we don't really have to because I feel like that'll make Jock come for us with both barrels. However, if we leave her behind, then he'd be mad, but he won't go so hard. But also, and this is where things get tricky." She took a deep breath and exhaled slowly.

"He has 400 thousand dollars tucked away, and I'm the only one besides him who has access to it. I want you looking good at all times, and myself as well. I wanna take everything he has before we leave and give you the money because I know you'll make it happen for us. What do you think?"

Gunz picked her up, looking her in the eyes. "I think it's time your boy became a boss. Let's take a few days and figure out how we gon' make all of this happen."

***

"The only reason I'm fronting you so much of my china is you've shown me you can handle it in large quantities. Even though your mouth is way too big for your position in the game, you're a hustler. In Miami, we gotta honor those who makes us rich. So, in those two bags are 20 kilos of heroin. Street value is 100 thousand dollars a piece. I want 150 thousand, and the other bag is another 20, but off of that, you give me 75 thousand. That's 225 thousand all together, with a time frame of one month, because that's all the time you need, am I correct?" Marvey said, looking Jock over closely.

His bloodshot eyes lowered into slits. His nephew rubbed him the wrong way. He knew that his arrogance would one day be his downfall. He was sure of that.

Jock picked up the big duffel bags and sat them on the back seat of his Navigator. He unzipped one and rifled through it, taking a silver pack into his hand and looking it over before zipping the bag back.

"I'll have yo' money in three weeks. Only a poor hustler would need a whole month to handle this lil' work. By the end of the month, I'm looking to run Atlanta. Now, let's talk about my white girl?"

Marvey nodded his head. "Fifteen a kee. I brought ten right now. You pay me by the end of the week, and that's 150 thousand."

Sane came over and gave Jock another duffel bag and went and stood behind Marvey, all while holding an AR-15, ready to wet some shit up. He didn't like Jock, and never had. He'd heard about how he got down, and how he had rose to power by pulling kick doors. He hated robbers, and hoped Jock fucked up soon so he could discipline him on behalf on the Zoes.

Jock grabbed the bag and tossed it into the back of his truck.

"150 for the white girl. 225 for the boy. I got you, and I'll be in touch about the white bitch in three days." He said, referring to the cocaine. Marvey nodded.

***

Babygirl came out of the bathroom and almost ran right into Jahrome. He stopped short and spilled some of his cereal out of his bowl. "Dang, my bad, sis."

"Naw, that was my fault," she said, rushing into the bathroom to get a bundle of tissue, before leaning down and wiping up the small mess of Crunch Berries. After she wiped it up, she continued on her way down the hall until he called her name.

"Babygirl, let me holla at you real fast in here." He said, stepping into the bathroom. They had been walking on egg shells around one another for three days straight. He felt like they needed to talk about it.

Babygirl reluctantly turned around and followed him into the bathroom. She hoped he wasn't getting ready to scold her.

As soon as she stepped in, Jahrome closed the door and looked her up and down. She refused to look up at him, and that made him feel uncomfortable.

He took her chin and tilted her head upward so she could look at him. "Talk to me, sis. What's going on inside of your mind, honestly?"

Babygirl lowered her head. She felt confused and alone. "Um, I guess I just…" She stopped and took a deep breath, losing her ability to speak to a man she had known her entire life. She had always felt confident around her brother until recently. Now, she felt shy and unable to be her normal self. She didn't want to upset him, or make a fool of herself.

He grabbed her face into his hands, and kissed her on the forehead, before looking into her eyes. He rubbed her soft cheek, right along the scar. "Talk to me, beautiful. You know you're my everything, and I'm here for you first and foremost, until my last breath. You can tell me anything, because I need to know what's going on inside." He said, pointing his finger softly to her chest.

Babygirl felt like she wanted to melt. She took another deep breath and tried to focus. Exhaling slowly, she calmed herself down. "Okay, now I just want you to listen to me without judging, and we'll go from there. Can you do that?" She looked him over closely. "Wait, first of all, where is Mami?" She asked.

"She had to run some errands. She'll be back in an hour or so, but that's not important. Tell me what's on your heart."

She lowered her head and shook it. "Jahrome, I need you in a way I have never needed you before." She blinked and tears fell down her cheeks. She was silent for a long time. He brushed her hair out of her face and rubbed her cheek again.

"Talk to me, sis. Tell me what you're feeling. I'm here for you." He kissed her on the forehead and tilted her chin upward so she could look into his hazel eyes.

Babygirl smiled weakly and lowered her gaze again. The sight of his handsome face was driving her crazy. Her brother looked like a cuter version of Shemar Moore. What made him look better was his dimples and his deep waves. She couldn't understand why she was even having those thoughts. She shook her head hard.

"Look, Jahrome, I find myself needing you more and more each day. I feel so alone and abandoned in this world ever since this crap happened to me. I feel ugly, and I feel like nobody could ever want me again." Tears dripped out of her eyes. "I feel like a burden to you and Mami, and I hate being that way, but I can't help it. I need you, and I don't want to share you with her. I want you to love me like you love her. I want you to want me in the same way that you want her. I mean in every single way, because I will be everything you need me to be. I love you, and I will always cherish you, Jahrome." She whimpered, and shook her head, before sinking to the floor of the bathroom.

"I know it isn't right. I know I'm not supposed to look at you like that, but I can't help it. You are looking a broken, damaged, and abused woman. I'm lost, and you're the only man I know who will search to find me. You'll restore me, and find a way to pick me up, before I take myself out of the game."

Jahrome slumped down to his knees at hearing the last part, and pulled her into his arms, kissing her forehead, and holding her tight. "Babygirl, are you saying that you've been thinking about taking your life?"

She was quiet for a while, before nodding. "Yeah, I've been thinking about that a lot." She said with her voice breaking up. Her face was wet with tears.

Jahrome kissed her wet cheek and held her as tight as he could. Now tears were rolling down his cheeks. He imagined his sister taking her own life, and it broke his heart.

For as long as he had been alive, she had been there for him. She had been his strength through the good and bad times. They had made it together. There was nothing in the world that he wouldn't do for her, and when he imagined life without her, it was way too much to bear. He needed her just as much as she needed him.

He held her face in his hands, leaned in and kissed her lips softly. "Babygirl, I'll die without you. You are my everything, and the strongest part of me. This world means absolutely nothing to me if you ain't in it. So, I never want to hear you say you want me to love you like I love somebody else, because I can never love anybody even a piece as much as I love you. You understand that?"

She felt her heart skip a beat. She closed her eyes and nodded. "Yes."

"And I will do anything for you. All you gotta do is tell me what ways you need me, and I got you. Blood is thicker than water, and you are always my first priority. Do you understand that?"

She shook her head, and more tears came down her cheeks. "But you don't understand what I'm saying, Jahrome. I'm saying I want you for me. Not as my brother, but as everything plus that." She shook her head harder. "I don't want nobody else but you. I'm scared of that world, and I just want to be in your arms as much as possible. I want you to love me harder. I want you to need me like I need you. I want your heart. I want your mind, body, and spirit. All of you.

That's why I'm so worried, because I know you won't give me that. And if I can't have that, then I don't want to be here, because not having all of you is killing me." She leaned forward and cried against his chest.

Jahrome felt defeated. He honestly didn't know what to do. He loved her with all of him, but what she was asking was a lot to carry. He had never really thought that far into things in regards to her because she was his sister. He was trying to make sense of everything.

He kissed her scar, and then her lips, sucking them enough to let her know that he was there for her. They felt soft and were little salty because of her tears. Babygirl wrapped her arms around his neck, and returned his kisses, sucking on his lips, and breathing heavily into his mouth. His lips were juicy, she opened her eyes briefly to see the tears rolling down his face.

She stood up, and he came up along with her. They crashed into the door, kissing and biting on each other's lips. Babygirl moaned and pulled him against her. Her breathing was quick.

Jahrome felt her breasts against his chest, and he decided to let his mind be all about healing her by any means. He no longer cared about what the world would think. His sole focus was making sure Babygirl was stronger afterward than when she'd first came to him. After all, he her loved more than anyone else in the whole world.

She pulled up his wife beater, exposing his well-developed chest and abs. She ran her hands over them, moaning deep within her throat, feeling an insatiable hunger for him. She kissed his chest first, and then sucked on it, rubbing his muscles hard, feeling the ripples under her hand, while he rubbed down her back and cupped her thick ass cheeks that peeked out of her pink boy short panties. He squeezed the globes before sucking on her neck.

"This is what you want, right?" He bit into her neck. "You want me like this. You want me to heal this body, right?" He asked, and slid his hand into her leg hole, rubbing over her bare kitty lips. The juices leaked on to his fingers, saturating them almost immediately.

Babygirl threw her head back and moaned loudly. "Please, Jahrome. Please, I'll do anything. I'm begging you to make love to me right now. I need you so bad." Never before in her life had she needed a man so bad. Never had she craved someone so hard. Jahrome was driving her crazy.

He knelt down, and pulled her panties down in one swift motion, all the way to her ankles, and spread her legs apart. The only thing going through his head was healing her. He wanted to make sure when all was said and done, she knew he would always be there for her.

Ghost

Chapter 17

Jahrome looked up to her from the floor, and blinked tears. "I just want you to know that I will do anything for you. You are my everything." She spread her legs further apart, and he eyed her kitty. He reached upward and rubbed her box, before spreading the lips apart. She saw him sticking his face into her middle, licking his lips. He was prepared to give her the pleasure that she craved.

As much as she wanted and needed it, she felt he had already proven himself to her. She thought the sex part of things could wait for another day. She truly just yearned to be in his arms, so she closed her thighs, putting a stop to his feast. "Jahrome, let's not. I love you. You are my life. I'm so sorry for how I need you. I can't help it." She wrapped her arms around his neck. "Can you hold me instead?"

Jahrome pulled her closer to him, and kissed her lips. Then, they heard the front door slam. They scrambled for their clothes.

Mami stumbled through the house. She bumped into the coffee table and fell to her knees, tears streaming down her cheeks. She could barely breathe. She had gotten the news that her brother had been found brutally murdered, and the reality was too much for her to handle.

She stood back up. "Jahrome! *Papi!* Where are you? I can't take this shit! I need you, *papi!*" She hollered before falling on to her stomach and curling into a ball.

Jahrome carne out of the bathroom and ran down the hall seeing Mami passed out on the floor.

He dropped to his knees right beside her and moved her curly hair out of her face. Her eyes were wide open, yet it felt like she was barely there. She looked like she was having a nervous breakdown.

Babygirl came and dropped down beside them as well. "What's the matter with her?" She asked, looking her over.

He shrugged his shoulders. "I don't know. She ain't said nothing yet. Baby, what's the matter? Talk to me." He rubbed her face and pulled her up to a sitting position.

She blinked, then her eyes opened wide again. "My brother is dead. They just found him and Mariella's body at her home. Both of their heads were blown off, and the house was ransacked. They're saying it had to be a robbery gone wrong, but it doesn't make sense because he never has drugs over his baby mother's house, so it couldn't have been about that. I'm so fucking hurt. I think I'm going crazy." She whimpered and started to shake, sobbing loudly.

Jahrome pulled her into his arms, and wiped away her tears, kissing her cheeks, and rocking with her as if she were a little child.

He felt bad for her, and at the same time, paranoid. Rico and Jahrome had been in some deep shit, and it was only a matter of time before things started to catch up to him.

Babygirl heard her phone ringing in the living room and got up to go grab it..

Jahrome kissed Mami again, and hugged her with his eyes closed, rocking her back and forth. "It's gon' be okay, baby. We'll get through this together. I'm here for you. Whatever we need to do, we'll do it. I got you."

Mami needed to hear those words. They were soothing and helped her to calm down. She was so thankful for him. So thankful to be in his arms. She closed her eyes, and imagined that she was a little baby girl, and he was her protector. He would never allow for anything to happen to her because she meant too much to him. He would make sure that she was always okay.

Babygirl dropped the phone. "Noooo! Noooo! Jahrome! Noooo!" She screamed and fell to her knees, with her mouth wide open. She walked all the way over to him on her knees, before falling against him. "Momma is dead. Our mother is dead. Somebody killed her, and Sister Robinson and Sister Patterson."

Jahrome saw his life flash before his eyes. He couldn't even fathom that reality of his mother being gone, and especially nobody killing her. He felt dizzy, but still he wrapped one arm around Mami, and the other around Babygirl. He knew he had to be strong for them, but inside, he felt so weak. He felt like he was ready to pass out. He was beyond lost.

* * *

"So I'll be back in a few hours. Make sure you finish cleaning up the rest of this house. Don't let me get back here and shit is still outta whack. You want me to fuck that ass?" Jock asked, mugging Dymond. He was irritated because he had been telling her for the last two days to get his crib in order, but the task had still not been completed. He didn't like telling her things more than once. It made him feel disrespected, and he wasn't having that shit in his house.

"No, daddy, I don't want you to do that. I'll get on top of everything and have it done before you get back. I'm sorry, my mind has just been--" She started before he cut her off.

"Bitch, I don't want to hear all of that. Just do like I say. You starting to get on my nerves though. Seems like you growing complacent. Don't have me replace yo' ass, especially with all them ghetto bitches fighting to take yo' slot. This shit getting old anyway." He mugged her, and shook his head before leaving out of the bedroom.

"Clean my house, or else." He threatened before going back down the stairs and leaving out the door.

Dymond peeked out of the upstairs window, and saw him getting into his truck. Aerial came running out of the house and knocked on his driver's side window. He rolled it down, and then opened the door. Aerial took a step back, and as soon she did, he got out and picked her up. She wrapped her legs around him, and he held her for a long while before kissing her cheeks. She could see his lips moving, and then, their daughter laid her head on his shoulder with her eyes closed. The sun shined on them, and they looked so happy together.

For some reason, it made Dymond feel sick to her stomach. Aerial was all he cared about. She felt like she was only his maid. It hurt her heart, but it gave her more motivation to carry out her plan.

He kissed Aerial's lips, and set her down, before getting back into his truck, and slowly backing down the driveway. He blew the horn one time, and Aerial waved at him, before he disappeared.

Dymond activated the tracking on her iPhone. When she saw the arrow pointed to their neighborhood, she knew she could track him successfully. She ran to the closet, and slid the double doors open, taking her clothes and pushing them to the side, then throwing the shoeboxes over her shoulders until she cleared the space where his secret safe was located. She pulled the rug back, and removed the wooden floorboards, until she saw the digital green face "Secure-lock" repeatedly. She took a deep breath and punched in the code, praying that he hadn't changed it.

After a series of beeps, the safe flashed from red to green, and said, "System disarmed." The door hissed, and then popped open. What she saw nearly made her faint. Jock had the safe stuffed with stacks and stacks of money. It looked to be more then she thought it was. She ran to her closet and grabbed a Gucci bag, and started to stuff it to the max with as much money as she could get into it.

She had a smile on her face, and tears coming down her cheeks. She was so happy. She felt like a slave who was getting their freedom papers. She knew the money meant a brand new start for her. A new beginning where she wouldn't have to worry about Jock running her life with an iron fist. Her destiny would be placed in her own hands, and she would be able to live happily with Gunz.

She wound up filling up both of her Gucci bags and half of a Birkin. She moved the night table out of the way that was on the side of their bed, and pulled the carpet back, going through the same process for another safe, when it popped up, she was shocked to see that it filled with silver packaged bricks. She remembered Gunz had told her to grab all of the dope, and the money, so they could have a fresh start in Miami. He said he had plans for them, and she believed it. She stuffed the Birkin, and then her Gucci luggage.

She didn't know what was in each package. All she knew was it meant a lot of money mixed with the cash they already had.

She was just zipping up the bag, when Aerial knocked on the door, and then opened it, causing her to knock over the bag of money. About twenty thousand spilled out across the floor.

Aerial came into the room, looked down and saw the money, and her eyes grew wide. "Oooh, why are you taking my dad's money?" She asked confused, already knowing that it couldn't have belonged to her mother.

At 9 years old, she was sharp. Jock always taught her as much as he could while he held her in his arms. He always told her if things ever looked fishy around the house and he wasn't there to call him right away, and he would tell her what was what. She was seconds away from calling him.

Dymond saw her daughter pull her phone out, and she damn near broke her neck to get over to her. Aerial turned her back and went down her call log until it highlighted the name, "Daddy." Then, she clicked on it before her mother tackled her to the floor and sent the phone flying across it.

"Heyyy! What's your problem?" Aerial whined, and tried to get up. Now she knew something was wrong, and she had to let her father know. She struggled to get to her feet, but her mother held her down by the shoulders.

"Baby, you don't understand what's going on here. Now, I need for you to calm down, and let Mommy explain something to you."

Aerial struggled to get up. She frowned her face, and tried to twist her way out, but it was useless. "Get off of me, Momma! I want to call my daddy!" She grunted.

Dymond already knew if she called Jock, her plans of happiness would be ruined. He would turn the truck around so fast, come home, and kill her for trying to rob him blind. Her heart beat faster in her chest.

"Get off of me right now! Let me up! I'm telling my father you're taking his money. You're going to be in trouble." She pumped her hips and tried to shake the woman off to no avail.

Dymond blinked back tears. "Please, just listen to me, baby. We have to get out of here before your daddy kills me. Please, just listen to me." She begged.

Aerial was a daddy's girl. She always had been since birth being that he spoiled her and showered her with unconditional love. She loved him ten times more than she loved Dymond, and she wasn't shy about admitting that. "I hate you, and I'm not going anywhere with you. I want to call my daddy! Now, bitch!" She jerked her hips, and tried to flip her off.

152

Dymond held her down and shook her head. Her heart hurt because she knew what she had to do, and she didn't want to do it. She prayed Aerial would just listen, that she would see things her way, but the little girl was too far gone.

"I hate you! I hate you! Why don't you just leave me and my daddy alone! Nobody loves you here! I'm telling him how you hurt me, and he's going to kick you-"

Dymond wrapped both hands around Aerial's neck and squeezed with all of her might. Tears ran down her cheeks, and she silently prayed in her head. She prayed for forgiveness, and prayed God understood that all she wanted was to be happy, and her daughter shouldn't have been given the power to stand in the way of that. She choked and choked, squeezing more and more tightly, taking the life out of her daughter.

Aerial swung at her mother's hands. Her eyes were opened wide, and she tried to do all she could to get loose. She couldn't breathe, and her chest felt like it was caving in. She wet herself, and continued to kick her legs. Dymond shook her head from right to left. "I'm so sorry, baby. I'm so, so sorry." She whimpered, killing her.

* * *

"Hello? Hello? Aerial?" Jock mugged his phone, shrugged his shoulders, before ending the call. He loved his daughter but he had money on his mind, and needed to get his bands up before his payment was due to the Haitians at the end of the week.

Ghost

Chapter 18

Jahrome took a deep breath, and watched as the mortician pulled the sheet backward, exposing his mother's mangled face. Him, Babygirl and Mami had arrived at the hospital to identify her body after they were informed of her death.

As soon as he saw it, he dropped to his knees in disbelief, and Babygirl kneeled to console him. He heard her sobbing next to him. His heart was torn in two.

He wrapped his arms around his sister as his phone vibrated on his hip. He didn't even have the strength to grab it.

Mami heard it, and took it from him, answering it. "Hello?"

Jock cleared his throat. "Tell that bitch ass nigga he and that bitch next." He ended the call.

Mami's eyes were as big as saucers. She didn't know what to think. "Some nigga said you and that bitch is next. I don't know if he was talking about Babygirl, or me. We gotta get the fuck out of Atlanta. Shit is getting too crazy."

Jahrome stood up and wiped his face. The image of his mother's dead body was fresh in his mind. "Naw, fuck that. I know who did this to my mother. I know it gotta be that nigga, Jock, and I refuse to let him get away with this shit. That nigga took my momma's life, all because of his punk ass brother. I ain't finna roll over and just let this shit happen. You gotta be crazy if you think that."

His chest rose and fell. He could feel his head becoming hot. He no longer cared about the consequences. Jock had crossed the line and did the unthinkable. He felt like he had to pay.

Mami lowered her head. "We still gotta bury my brother. Now, we're talking about going to war with crazy ass Jock, and them fools from Bankhead?" She looked from Babygirl to him. "Do you think that's who killed my brother, too? It wouldn't be no coincidence."

Jahrome could barely think straight. He was imagining going to war with Bankhead all by himself. He had a death wish. There was nothing about to stop him from avenging his mother's death.

"I don't know, but I'm finna go at that nigga like he did."

Mami nodded her head. "Well, I gotta call my uncle, and he'll get you right. He lives out in Lithonia, Georgia. He loved my brother, and if you feel like you wanna go at Jock and them fools, then he's going to make sure you have some killers around you. Let's get out of here. This place is giving me the creeps. No disrespect to your mother, of course." They both nodded in understanding.

Five minutes later, they were sitting in Mami's truck, and she was scrolling down her call log when there was a squealing of tires, and then the sounds of a car slamming on its brakes. *Errrr-urrh!*

Jahrome looked to his right and saw three masked dudes jump out of an all-black Escalade with assault rifles in their hands, and then gunfire erupted.

To Be Continued . . .
A Savage Dopeboy 2
Coming Soon

Submission Guideline

Submit the first three chapters of your completed manuscript to ldpsubmissions@gmail.com, subject line: Your book's title. The manuscript must be in a .doc file and sent as an attachment. Document should be in Times New Roman, double spaced and in size 12 font. Also, provide your synopsis and full contact information. If sending multiple submissions, they must each be in a separate email.

Have a story but no way to send it electronically? You can still submit to LDP/Ca$h Presents. Send in the first three chapters, written or typed, of your completed manuscript to:

LDP: Submissions Dept
Po Box 870494
Mesquite, Tx 75187

DO NOT send original manuscript. Must be a duplicate.

Provide your synopsis and a cover letter containing your full contact information.

Thanks for considering LDP and Ca$h Presents.

BOW DOWN TO MY GANGSTA

By **Ca$h**

TORN BETWEEN TWO

By **Coffee**

BLOOD STAINS OF A SHOTTA **III**

By **Jamaica**

STEADY MOBBIN **III**

By **Marcellus Allen**

BLOOD OF A BOSS **VI**

SHADOWS OF THE GAME II

By **Askari**

LOYAL TO THE GAME **IV**

By **T.J. & Jelissa**

A DOPEBOY'S PRAYER **II**

By **Eddie "Wolf" Lee**

IF LOVING YOU IS WRONG… **III**

By **Jelissa**

TRUE SAVAGE **VII**

MIDNIGHT CARTEL

DOPE BOY MAGIC

By **Chris Green**

BLAST FOR ME **III**

DUFFLE BAG CARTEL **IV**

HEARTLESS GOON **III**

A SAVAGE DOPEBOY II

By **Ghost**

A HUSTLER'S DECEIT III

KILL ZONE **II**

BAE BELONGS TO ME III

SOUL OF A MONSTER III

By **Aryanna**

THE COST OF LOYALTY **III**

By **Kweli**

THE SAVAGE LIFE II

By **J-Blunt**

KING OF NEW YORK V

COKE KINGS IV

BORN HEARTLESS II

By **T.J. Edwards**

GORILLAZ IN THE BAY V

De'Kari

THE STREETS ARE CALLING II

Duquie Wilson

KINGPIN KILLAZ IV

STREET KINGS III

PAID IN BLOOD III

CARTEL KILLAZ III

Hood Rich

SINS OF A HUSTLA II

ASAD

TRIGGADALE III

Elijah R. Freeman

KINGZ OF THE GAME V

Playa Ray

SLAUGHTER GANG IV

RUTHLESS HEART II

By Willie Slaughter

THE HEART OF A SAVAGE II

By Jibril Williams

FUK SHYT II

By Blakk Diamond

THE DOPEMAN'S BODYGAURD II

By Tranay Adams

TRAP GOD II

By Troublesome

YAYO II

A SHOOTER'S AMBITION II

By S. Allen

GHOST MOB

Stilloan Robinson

KINGPIN DREAMS

By Paper Boi Rari

CREAM

By Yolanda Moore

SON OF A DOPE FIEND II

By Renta

FOREVER GANGSTA II

By Adrian Dulan

A Savage Dopeboy

LOYALTY AIN'T PROMISED
By Keith Williams
THE PRICE YOU PAY FOR LOVE
By Destiny Skai
THE LIFE OF A HOOD STAR
By Rashia Wilson
TOE TAGZ II
By Ah'Million

<u>Available Now</u>

RESTRAINING ORDER **I & II**
By **CA$H & Coffee**
LOVE KNOWS NO BOUNDARIES **I II & III**
By **Coffee**
RAISED AS A GOON I, II, III & IV
BRED BY THE SLUMS I, II, III
BLAST FOR ME I & II
ROTTEN TO THE CORE I II III
A BRONX TALE I, II, III
DUFFEL BAG CARTEL I II III
HEARTLESS GOON
A SAVAGE DOPEBOY
HEARTLESS GOON I II
By **Ghost**
LAY IT DOWN **I & II**
LAST OF A DYING BREED

Ghost

BLOOD STAINS OF A SHOTTA I & II
By **Jamaica**
LOYAL TO THE GAME
LOYAL TO THE GAME II
LOYAL TO THE GAME III
LIFE OF SIN I, II III
By **TJ & Jelissa**
BLOODY COMMAS I & II
SKI MASK CARTEL I II & III
KING OF NEW YORK I II,III IV
RISE TO POWER I II III
COKE KINGS I II III
BORN HEARTLESS
By **T.J. Edwards**
IF LOVING HIM IS WRONG…I & II
LOVE ME EVEN WHEN IT HURTS I II III
By **Jelissa**
WHEN THE STREETS CLAP BACK I & II III
By **Jibril Williams**
A DISTINGUISHED THUG STOLE MY HEART I II & III
LOVE SHOULDN'T HURT I II III IV
RENEGADE BOYS I II III IV
By **Meesha**
A GANGSTER'S CODE I &, II III
A GANGSTER'S SYN I II III
THE SAVAGE LIFE
By **J-Blunt**

A Savage Dopeboy

PUSH IT TO THE LIMIT

By **Bre' Hayes**

BLOOD OF A BOSS **I, II, III, IV, V**

SHADOWS OF THE GAME

By **Askari**

THE STREETS BLEED MURDER **I, II & III**

THE HEART OF A GANGSTA I II& III

By **Jerry Jackson**

CUM FOR ME

CUM FOR ME 2

CUM FOR ME 3

CUM FOR ME 4

CUM FOR ME 5

An **LDP Erotica Collaboration**

BRIDE OF A HUSTLA **I II & II**

THE FETTI GIRLS **I, II& III**

CORRUPTED BY A GANGSTA I, II III, IV

BLINDED BY HIS LOVE

By **Destiny Skai**

WHEN A GOOD GIRL GOES BAD

By **Adrienne**

THE COST OF LOYALTY I II

By Kweli

A GANGSTER'S REVENGE **I II III & IV**

THE BOSS MAN'S DAUGHTERS

THE BOSS MAN'S DAUGHTERS II

THE BOSSMAN'S DAUGHTERS III

Ghost

A Savage Dopeboy

By **CATO**

THE ULTIMATE BETRAYAL

By **Phoenix**

BOSS'N UP **I , II & III**

By **Royal Nicole**

I LOVE YOU TO DEATH

By Destiny J

I RIDE FOR MY HITTA

I STILL RIDE FOR MY HITTA

By **Misty Holt**

LOVE & CHASIN' PAPER

By **Qay Crockett**

TO DIE IN VAIN

SINS OF A HUSTLA

By **ASAD**

BROOKLYN HUSTLAZ

By **Boogsy Morina**

BROOKLYN ON LOCK I & II

By **Sonovia**

GANGSTA CITY

By **Teddy Duke**

A DRUG KING AND HIS DIAMOND I & II III

A DOPEMAN'S RICHES

HER MAN, MINE'S TOO I, II

CASH MONEY HO'S

By Nicole Goosby

TRAPHOUSE KING **I II & III**

Ghost

KINGPIN KILLAZ I II III
STREET KINGS I II
PAID IN BLOOD **I II**
CARTEL KILLAZ I II
By **Hood Rich**
LIPSTICK KILLAH **I, II, III**
CRIME OF PASSION I & II
By **Mimi**
STEADY MOBBN' **I, II, III**
By **Marcellus Allen**
WHO SHOT YA **I, II, III**
SON OF A DOPE FIEND
Renta
GORILLAZ IN THE BAY **I II III IV**
DE'KARI
TRIGGADALE I II
Elijah R. Freeman
GOD BLESS THE TRAPPERS I, II, III
THESE SCANDALOUS STREETS I, II, III
FEAR MY GANGSTA I, II, III
THESE STREETS DON'T LOVE NOBODY I, II
BURY ME A G I, II, III, IV, V
A GANGSTA'S EMPIRE I, II, III, IV
THE DOPEMAN'S BODYGAURD
Tranay Adams
THE STREETS ARE CALLING
Duquie Wilson

MARRIED TO A BOSS... I II III

By Destiny Skai & Chris Green

KINGZ OF THE GAME I II III IV

Playa Ray

SLAUGHTER GANG I II III

RUTHLESS HEART

By Willie Slaughter

THE HEART OF A SAVAGE

By Jibril Williams

FUK SHYT

By Blakk Diamond

DON'T F#CK WITH MY HEART I II

By Linnea

ADDICTED TO THE DRAMA I II III

By Jamila

YAYO

A SHOOTER'S AMBITION

By S. Allen

TRAP GOD

By Troublesome

FOREVER GANGSTA

By Adrian Dulan

TOE TAGZ

By Ah'Million

BOOKS BY LDP'S CEO, CA$H

TRUST IN NO MAN

TRUST IN NO MAN 2

TRUST IN NO MAN 3

BONDED BY BLOOD

SHORTY GOT A THUG

THUGS CRY

THUGS CRY 2

THUGS CRY 3

TRUST NO BITCH

TRUST NO BITCH 2

TRUST NO BITCH 3

TIL MY CASKET DROPS

RESTRAINING ORDER

RESTRAINING ORDER 2

IN LOVE WITH A CONVICT

Coming Soon

BONDED BY BLOOD 2

BOW DOWN TO MY GANGSTA

A Savage Dopeboy

www.ingramcontent.com/pod-product-compliance
Lightning Source LLC
Chambersburg PA
CBHW051225260626
47161CB00005BA/1691